THE GREYHOUND OF THE BASKERVILLES

ARTHUR CONAN DOYLE
(AND SOME NEW BITS BY JOHN
GASPARD)

ALBERT'S BRIDGE
BOOKS

The Greyhound of the Baskervilles

First Edition | 2019

Albert's Bridge Books

Printed in the United States of America

For Tim.

"Dogs don't make mistakes."

The Case-Book of Sherlock Holmes
Arthur Conan Doyle

PREFACE

What follows is Arthur Conan Doyle's classic mystery, "The Hound of the Baskervilles."

Mostly.

It's the same characters, the same action, and much of the same dialogue.

What's different?

Well, it's a little shorter, a little leaner, a little less verbose in some sections.

But the chief difference is that it's now narrated by a dog.

A greyhound, in fact, named Septimus.

In the following pages, he tells his story of how he became "The Greyhound of the Baskervilles."

So settle in.

And enjoy.

CHAPTER 1

*M*r. Sherlock Holmes, who was usually very late in the mornings, save upon those not infrequent occasions when he was up all night, was seated at the breakfast table.

I lay upon the hearth-rug and aimlessly champed on the stick which a visitor had left behind the night before. It was a fine, thick piece of wood, bulbous-headed, and it exhibited a fine, earthy flavor. I am not often afforded the opportunity to gnaw on objects of any kind, as it is usually frowned upon here in 221b Baker Street. So I was truly enjoying this rare moment of woody pleasure.

As I chomped, I noticed, just under the head of the stick, was a broad silver band nearly an inch across. "To James Mortimer, M.R.C.S., from his friends of the C.C.H.," was engraved upon it, along with the date "1884."

"Well, what do you make of it?"

Holmes was sitting with his back to me, and—to the best of my knowledge—I had given him no sign of my occupation.

"How the devil did he know what I was doing?" I thought, dropping the cane at once and affecting an air of innocence I was

1

convinced I wasn't actually pulling off. Then I heard the voice of Dr. Watson, next to me.

"I believe you have eyes in the back of your head," he said.

"Ah," I thought. "Watson must have been looking at the stick as well."

"Perhaps. I also have a well-polished, silver-plated coffee-pot in front of me," said Holmes. "But, tell me, Watson, what do you make of our visitor's stick?"

"You mean the one your hound has been so ardently biting upon?" asked Watson.

"On the contrary, Septimus has been carefully probing the item to better determine its provenance."

"Yes, well, to my untrained eye, he appears to be chewing on it."

"There is, Watson, a thin line between mastication and investigation," offered Holmes in my defense. "Now, since we have been so unfortunate as to miss our unknown guest and have no notion of his errand, this accidental souvenir becomes of importance. Let me hear you reconstruct the man by an examination of it."

Watson bent down to pick up my new-found treasure, which I allowed him to do without the slightest of growls. That sort of thing, in the greyhound breed, is just not done. We may be athletes, but we are also gentlemen, to a man. We are known for our pleasant, warm natures and I felt this was not the moment to tarnish that well-won reputation.

"I think," said Watson in what I took to be an imitation of the methods of my companion, "that Dr. Mortimer is a successful, elderly medical man, well-esteemed since those who know him give him this mark of their appreciation."

"Good!" said Holmes. "Excellent!"

I wasn't in strict agreement with Watson's assessment, but I let the good doctor continue, as I realized that no one had, in point of fact, requested my opinion on this matter.

"I think," continued Watson, "that there is also the probability of his being a country practitioner who does a great deal of his visiting on foot."

"Why so?" asked Holmes, which was surprising, as it was the very question which had occurred to me. He gave me a quick glance and a smile, suggesting we were—once again—both on the same deductive track.

"Because this stick, though originally a very handsome one, has been so knocked about that I can hardly imagine a town practitioner carrying it. The thick-iron ferrule is worn down, so it is evident that he has done a great amount of walking with it."

I was pleased to note that he made no mention of the one or two small gouges I had inadvertently made to the cane during my brief perusal of the object.

"Perfectly sound!" said Holmes, although I could tell from his tone that he thought nothing of the kind. I'm sure my face registered this confusion, although neither of the humans seemed to notice it.

"And then again, there is the 'friends of the C.C.H.' I should guess that to be the Something Something Hunt, the local hunt to whose members he has possibly given some surgical assistance, and which has made him a small presentation in return."

"Really, Watson, you excel yourself," said Holmes, pushing back his chair and lighting a cigarette. He glanced down at me and offered the slightest of winks in my direction. I am not capable of returning that unique gesticulation, so I simply nodded in understanding.

"I am bound to say that in all the accounts which you have been so good as to give of my own small achievements, you have habitually underrated your own abilities," continued Holmes. "It may be that you are not yourself luminous, but you are a conductor of light. Some people without possessing genius have a remarkable power of stimulating it. I confess, my dear fellow, that I am very much in your debt."

He had never said as much before, and I must admit that his

words seemed to give Dr. Watson something akin to keen plea-sure. I am not always correct in my assessment of human facial expressions, but the kindly doctor was clearly pleased by some-thing and I don't think I was taking too much of a logical leap to assume it was in response to my master's fulsome comments.

Holmes then took the stick from the doctor's hands and exam-ined it for a few minutes with his naked eyes. Then with an expression of interest, he laid down his cigarette and carried the cane to the window. Intrigued, I got up and followed him, leaning heavily against his leg once I had arrived. He patted my head absently as he looked over the stick again, this time with the precision offered by a convex lens.

"Interesting, though elementary," he said. "There are certainly one or two indications upon the stick, as I'm sure Septimus observed. It gives us the basis for several deductions."

He returned to his favorite corner of the settee, while I re-settled myself neatly upon the hearth-rug.

"Has anything escaped me?" asked Watson with some self-importance. "I trust that there is nothing of consequence which I have overlooked?"

I glanced up at Holmes expectantly, wondering how he planned to deliver his assessment of Watson's sad attempt at deduction.

"I am afraid, my dear Watson, that most of your conclusions were erroneous. When I said that you stimulated me, I meant, to be frank, that in noting your fallacies I was occasionally guided towards the truth. Not that you are entirely wrong in this instance. The man is certainly a country practitioner. And he walks a good deal."

"Then I was right."

"To that extent."

"But that was all?"

"No, no, my dear Watson, not all—by no means all."

Holmes was being kind. Watson was mostly wrong.

To be honest, at that point my attention toward their conversation waned, as I reflected back on a hare Holmes and I had spotted during a recent excursion through Hyde Park. I had made a mental note to revisit the event, and this seemed like an ideal time to reflect upon it. However, I suspect that while I was in my reverie, Holmes corrected the poor doctor on several key deficits within his deduction.

For example, a presentation of a gift, such as a walking stick, to a doctor was more likely to come from a hospital than from a hunt. And when the initials 'C.C.' are placed before the word hospital, the name 'Charing Cross' very naturally suggests itself.

It was not, I also considered, unreasonable to infer that the gift came at the time when this Dr. Mortimer withdrew from the service of the hospital in order to start a practice for himself. I could think of no other reason to give such a stick to a human. As I tuned back into their conversation, it became clear that Holmes and I had headed down the same deductive path.

"Now, you will observe that he could not have been on the staff of the hospital, since only a man well-established in a London practice could hold such a position, and such a one would not drift into the country. What was he, then?"

Watson seemed to conclude the question was rhetorical, although the answer seemed obvious to me: If he was in the hospital and yet not on the staff, he could only have been a house-surgeon or a house-physician.

"He was little more than a senior student," continued Holmes. "And he left five years ago—the date is on the stick."

I nodded in complete agreement.

In my mind, the middle-aged family practitioner described by Dr. Watson vanished into thin air and instead emerged as a young fellow, under thirty, amiable, unambitious, absent-minded, and the possessor of a favorite dog, which I would describe—if pressed on the matter—as roughly being larger than a terrier and smaller than a mastiff. Of course, no one was asking me.

I heard Dr. Watson laugh incredulously and assumed Sherlock Holmes had offered up a similar accounting. I looked up in time to observe him as he leaned back in his settee and blew little wavering rings of smoke up to the ceiling. I am no fan of his smoking, one of several of his human habits with which I could do without. But such is the lot of a house guest, whether two or four-legged. It is, after all, his home.

"As to the latter part, I have no means of checking you," Watson said, "but at least it is not difficult to find out a few particulars about the man's age and professional career."

From his small medical book shelf, he took down a book and began to page through it.

"Mortimer, James, M.R.C.S., 1882, Grimpen, Dartmoor, Devon," Watson read, glancing up to see if he still held Holmes' attention. "House-surgeon, from 1882 to 1884, at Charing Cross Hospital."

He went on to read more detail about the young doctor and his career, all of which sailed over my head. I glanced over toward my food bowl, wondering—not for the first time this morning—if I had in fact finished everything in it. Part of me was sure I had, while there was an inkling deep within my brain which suggested there could easily be one or two more morsels remaining. The only way to solve this mystery, I reasoned, was to head back to my food bowl to investigate. Which I did.

"No mention of that local hunt, Watson," I heard Holmes say with what sounded like a mischievous smile, "but he is a country doctor, as you very astutely observed. I think that I am fairly justified in my inferences."

"And the dog?" Watson asked.

I looked up from my bowl, which sadly was empty, to see which dog it was to which they were referring. Since neither man was looking my way, I assumed they must have been discussing the dog belonging to Dr. Mortimer. Clearly Holmes had come to the same conclusion I had, although now I was curious to hear if he had been able to narrow the breed as astutely.

"The dog has been in the habit of carrying this stick behind his master," Holmes said. "Being a heavy stick, the dog has held it tightly by the middle, and the marks of his teeth are very plainly visible."

"Well, yes," Watson said morosely, then added, "But Septimus here was just gnawing on that same stick. How do you know he didn't leave the markings?"

Holmes glanced at me and we shared a quick smile. He had risen and paced the room as he spoke. And, as was my habit, I fell in step beside him. Then he halted in the recess of the window and I nearly collided with him—also not an uncommon occurrence.

"The dog's jaw, as shown in the space between these marks, is too broad in my opinion for a terrier and yet not broad enough for a greyhound, or for that matter, a mastiff. It may have been— yes, by Jove, it is a curly-haired spaniel."

If I possessed the power of speech, I swear I would have uttered the same words at the exact same time, for my position by the window afforded me the same view as Holmes. Albeit, two or three feet lower.

Dr. Watson was shaking his head across the room. "My dear fellow, how can you possibly be so sure of that?"

"For the very simple reason that I see the dog himself on our very door-step. And there is the ring of its owner."

At that moment, I heard the chime of the bell and moved quickly to the door, to assist in any manner necessary the entrance of what was likely to be a fascinating guest. Anyone who travels with a dog immediately warrants my highest curiosity.

I looked upon the closed door in rapt anticipation. Now was the dramatic moment of fate, when you hear a step upon the stair which is walking into your life, and you know not whether for good or ill. I panted in anticipation. What does Dr. James

7

Mortimer, the man of science, ask of Sherlock Holmes, the specialist in crime? And what will be the disposition of his dog, the aforementioned curly-haired spaniel? I could hardly wait to discover and I suspect the rapid wagging of my tail revealed to all my intense interest in our visitor and his dog.

"Come in!"

The appearance of our visitor was a surprise to me, since I'd had precious few encounters with spaniels, curly-haired or otherwise.

First, it must be noted that the dog's hair was, indeed, curly. As a short-haired breed myself, I often marvel at the longer-haired varieties, burdened as they are with an excess of hair across their entire form. While I imagine it can be a comfort on the cold nights of winter, it hardly seems a fair exchange, for it must feel like hades itself in the aptly-named dogs days of summer.

The spaniel was curious but respectful, understanding he was entering a fresh environment, one upon which he held no claim. As a result, he proceeded cautiously into the room. Once he had judged I was just as inquisitive of him as he was of me, we moved into our traditional greeting format, which I find to be far more instructive than the odd human habit of grasping hands. In a matter of moments, we each had taken stock of the other and found no grounds upon which to quarrel. He moved back to his master, while I re-took my position upon the hearth-rug.

It was then I made my first appraisal of the human. He was a very tall, thin man, with a long nose like a beak, which jutted out between two keen eyes, set closely together and sparkling brightly from behind a pair of glasses.

He was clad in a professional but rather slovenly fashion, for his frock-coat was dingy and his trousers frayed. Though young, his long back was already bowed, and he walked with a forward thrust of his head and a general air of peering benevolence—not unlike an afghan hound or a swayed-back pony.

When he entered, his eyes had fallen upon the stick in

Holmes's hand, and he'd run towards it with an exclamation of joy.

"I am so very glad," said he. "I was not sure whether I had left it here or in the Shipping Office. I would not lose that stick for the world."

"A presentation, I see," said Holmes.

"Yes, sir."

"From Charing Cross Hospital?"

"From one or two friends there. On the occasion of my marriage."

"Dear, dear, that's bad!" said Holmes, shaking his head. He glanced down at me and I turned away in embarrassment. I could not meet his eyes nor he mine.

Dr. Mortimer blinked through his glasses in mild astonishment. "Why was it bad?"

"Only that you have disarranged our little deductions. Your marriage, you say?"

"Yes, sir. I married, and so left the hospital, and with it all hopes of a consulting practice. It was necessary to make a home of my own."

"Come, come, we are not so far wrong, after all," said Holmes, once again smiling upon me. I felt better, but still experienced the bitter sting of having been so clearly led astray in one false, yet elemental deduction.

"And now, Dr. James Mortimer—" Holmes continued.

"Mister, sir, Mister—a humble M.R.C.S."

"And a man of precise mind, evidently."

"A dabbler in science, Mr. Holmes, a picker up of shells on the shores of the great unknown ocean. I presume that it is Mr. Sherlock Holmes whom I am addressing and not—"

"No, this is my friend Dr. Watson."

"Glad to meet you, sir," he said.

I was not surprised or even annoyed to having been left out of this initial round of introductions. Unlike Watson and Holmes, I prefer to stay in the background, make my observations, and then step into the limelight only when the proper moment arises. To that end, I put my head down, closed my eyes and listened to the conversation as it unfolded in front of me.

"You interest me very much, Mr. Holmes," continued Mortimer. "I had hardly expected so dolichocephalic a skull or such well-marked supra-orbital development. Would you have any objection to my running my finger along your parietal fissure? A cast of your skull, sir, until the original is available, would be an ornament to any anthropological museum. It is not my intention to be fulsome, but I confess that I covet your skull."

I opened one eye, to determine if Holmes had tolerated the requested physical inspection. Humans, I thought not for the first time, are an odd breed. Sherlock Holmes, who I believe shared my sentiments, waved our strange visitor into a chair.

"You are an enthusiast in your line of thought, I perceive, sir, as I am in mine," said he. "I observe from your forefinger that you make your own cigarettes. Have no hesitation in lighting one."

The man drew out paper and tobacco and twirled the one up in the other with surprising dexterity. He had long, quivering fingers as agile and restless as the antennae of an insect. They reminded me of a bug I had eaten earlier in the week; I am not entirely aware of its particular genus, but I do remember it was tasty and offered a delightfully crunchy dining experience.

Holmes was silent, but his little darting glances showed me the interest which he took in our curious companion. An interest which I shared, but honestly not to the same degree as he.

Holmes lived for these sorts of encounters, while I would be just as happy to spend that same amount of time and effort napping. Experience has taught me that human problems always came down, in the end, to the most mundane of solutions. Greed, jealousy, lust, wrath. If it wasn't one, it was likely two or three or all of them.

"I presume, sir," said Holmes at last, "that it was not merely for the purpose of examining my skull that you have done me the honor to call here last night and again today? Kindly, tell me plainly what is the exact nature of the problem in which you demand my assistance?"

I yawned deeply, sure that what would follow would be a long recitation concerning petty human foibles and the like—crime, deception, lies—with hardly anything of interest to a perceptive greyhound such as myself.

As I was soon to discover, I could not have been more mistaken.

CHAPTER 2

"*I* have in my pocket a manuscript," said Dr. James Mortimer.

"I observed it as you entered the room," replied Holmes.

"It is an old manuscript."

"Early eighteenth century, unless it is a forgery."

"How can you say that, sir?"

"You have presented an inch or two of it to my examination all the time that you have been talking. It would be a poor expert who could not give the date of a document within a decade or so. You may possibly have read my little monograph upon the subject. I put your document at 1730."

"The exact date is 1742."

I have often admired Holmes' skill in matters such as this: the recognition of human-made objects and his ability to place them within a specific timeframe. I have similar skills, which are best (and rarely, more's the pity) applied to items in the natural world, many of which I am often sad to discover have been haphazardly discarded. At some future time, I hope to compose my own monograph on the hidden treasures found within the common dustbin. However, I am rarely allowed to conduct the necessary research and am frequently reprimanded for any attempt I might make.

Dr. Mortimer drew the document from his breast- pocket. "This family paper was committed to my care by Sir Charles Baskerville, whose sudden and tragic death some three months ago created so much excitement in Devonshire."

Holmes stretched out his hand for the manuscript and flattened it upon his knee. "You will observe, Watson, the alternative use of the long *s* and the short. It is one of several indications which enabled me to fix the date."

While I was hopeless when it came to dates, my olfactory senses told me the document had recently sat alongside a cut of beef, perhaps a roast of some sort. There was also the aroma, faint though it was, of roasted potatoes and perhaps a hint of garlic. I sniffed the air, but no further clues were forthcoming.

I thought again of my food bowl and its sad emptiness. While Holmes was an expert on fixing the dates of objects, he could be quite lax on remembering to feed me. If it were not for the occasional ministrations of our landlady, Mrs. Hudson, I felt it entirely possible that I might one day starve.

Watson looked over Holmes' shoulder at the yellow paper and the faded script which was holding their attention far better than it was holding mine. "Baskerville Hall," he said quietly. "1742."

"It appears to be a statement of some sort."

"Yes, it is a statement of a certain legend which runs in the Baskerville family," explained Mortimer.

"But I understand that it is something more modern and practical upon which you wish to consult me?"

"Most modern. A most practical, pressing matter, which must be decided within the next twenty-four hours. But the manuscript is short and is intimately connected with the affair. With your permission I will read it to you."

Holmes, with an air of resignation, leaned back in his chair, placed his finger-tips together, and closed his eyes. Dr. Mortimer turned the manuscript to the light as I lowered my head and shut my own eyes.

While I held a mild interest in what he was about to read, I was also willing to succumb to the pleasures of a mid-morning nap, if it happened upon me. I left the two options—listen to Dr. Mortimer or slip into sleep—as one would the result of a casual flip of a coin. At this very moment, it could go either direction.

Mortimer began in a high, cracking voice the following curious, old-world narrative, reading slowly from the document, which made an annoying crinkling sound in his hands.

"Of the origin of the Hound of the Baskervilles there have been many statements, yet as I come in a direct line from Hugo Baskerville, I have set it down with all belief that it occurred even as is here set forth.

"Know then that in the time of the Great Rebellion, this Manor of Baskerville was held by Hugo of that name, nor can it be gainsaid that he was a most wild, profane, and godless man.

"It chanced that this Hugo came to love the daughter of a yeoman who held lands near the Baskerville estate. But the young maiden, being discreet and of good repute, would ever avoid him, for she feared his evil name. So it came to pass that one Michaelmas this Hugo, with five or six of his idle and wicked companions, stole down upon the farm and carried off the maiden, her father and brothers being from home, as he well knew."

I'll be strictly honest with you. It was around this point in the story when sleep overtook me. I don't know how long I was in deep slumber, but when I awoke Dr. Mortimer was still reading from the weathered document.

I was able to gather from the context of his words that the kidnapping of the young maiden had not gone as planned. She must have escaped and a chase across the moors ensued, with Hugo following her on his horse. I stretched my legs at the thought of a nice long run, although I was not familiar with the concept of moors and wasn't entirely sure they were ideal for the sort of coursing I enjoyed.

Dr. Mortimer continued reading the tale:

"But at some length the whole of them, thirteen in number, took horse and started in pursuit. The moon shone clear above them, and they rode swiftly abreast, taking that path which the maid must needs have taken if she were to reach her own home.

"They had gone a mile or two when they passed one of the night shepherds upon the moorlands, and they cried to him to know if he had seen the hunt. And the man, as the story goes, was so crazed with fear that he could scarce speak, but at last he said 'Hugo Baskerville passed me upon his black mare, and there ran mute behind him such a hound of hell as God forbid should ever be at my heels.'"

Not so surprisingly, my ears perked up at this. The hound in question must not be a greyhound, I mused, for it was well known within the canine world that if any dog could outrace a horse, it would be a greyhound. I missed the next few moments from Mortimer's story while I considered how I might fare in my current condition against a horse in a direct, one-to-one competition. I fear that laziness and inactivity may have taken the sharp edges off my speed, but I still believe I could best all but the fastest of horses in a short sprint. I say this with all humility.

"The moon was shining bright upon the clearing, and there in the center lay the unhappy maid where she had fallen, dead of fear and of fatigue. But it was not the sight of her body, nor yet was it that of the body of Hugo Baskerville lying near her, which raised the hair upon the heads of these three dare-devil revelers. Standing over Hugo, and plucking at his throat, there stood a foul thing, a great, black beast, shaped like a hound, yet larger than any hound that ever mortal eye has rested upon.

"And even as they looked, the thing tore the throat out of Hugo Baskerville, on which, as it turned its blazing eyes and dripping jaws upon them, the men shrieked with fear and rode for dear life, still screaming, across the moor. One, it is said, died that very night of what he had seen, and the other twain were but broken men for the rest of their days."

I can't speak for Holmes or Watson, but this was certainly one of the finest stories it had ever been my good fortune to hear recounted before me.

It is not often, believe me, when a mere dog becomes the hero of a human's story. From time to time there are tales of a mutt pulling a baby from a well or signaling to homeowners that their homestead was ablaze. But in my limited literary experience, dogs are generally mere bit players, used for comic or charming effect and often have little or no impact on the dramatic thrust of the story. While that has not been the case in my adventures with Mr. Holmes, I fear it was the rule in other instances. But not in this fine story. I lifted my ears to ensure I did not miss one syllable of its climax.

"Such is the tale, my sons, of the coming of the hound which is said to have plagued the family so sorely ever since. Nor can it be denied that many of the family have been unhappy in their deaths, which have been sudden, bloody, and mysterious. To that Providence, my sons, I hereby commend you, and I counsel you by way of caution to forbear from crossing the moor in those dark hours when the powers of evil are exalted."

When Dr. Mortimer had finished reading this singular narrative, he pushed his spectacles up on his forehead and stared across at Mr. Sherlock Holmes. The latter yawned and tossed the end of his cigarette into the fire. Seeing him yawn, I too was overtaken by the desire to yawn. I noticed that the spaniel was also a victim of this yawning effect. Dr. Watson, to his credit, suppressed the desire, but I could see it took no small effort on his part.

"Well?" said Holmes.

"Do you not find it interesting?" asked Mortimer.

"To a collector of fairy tales," replied Holmes. Had he put the question to me, I can assure you my reaction would have been far more enthusiastic.

Had I the power of speech, my first question to the gentleman would have been to request another similar story about murderous hounds. If that were not available, then I would have requested a quick re-reading of the one he had just presented. I wagged my tail enthusiastically to register my admiration of the saga, but he did not seem to notice.

Instead, Dr. Mortimer drew a folded newspaper out of his pocket.

"Now, Mr. Holmes, we will give you something a little more recent. This is the Devon County Chronicle of May 14th of this year. It is a short account of the facts elicited at the death of Sir Charles Baskerville, which occurred a few days before that date."

My master leaned a little forward and his expression became intent. Our visitor readjusted his glasses and began to read again. I hoped against hope that this too was another story of a murderous hound.

"The recent sudden death of Sir Charles Baskerville has cast a gloom over the county. Though Sir Charles had resided at Baskerville Hall for a comparatively short period, his amiability of character and extreme generosity had won the affection and respect of all who had been brought into contact with him. It is only two years since he took up his residence at Baskerville Hall, and it is common talk how large were those schemes of reconstruction and improvement which have been interrupted by his death. Being himself childless, it was his openly expressed desire that the whole countryside should, within his own lifetime, profit by his good fortune, and many will have personal reasons for bewailing his untimely end.

"The circumstances connected with the death of Sir Charles cannot be said to have been entirely cleared up by the inquest, but at least enough has been done to dispose of those rumors to which local superstition has given rise. There is no reason whatever to suspect foul play, or to imagine that death could be from any but natural causes.

"Sir Charles was a widower, and a man who may be said to have been in some ways of an eccentric habit of mind. In spite of his considerable wealth he was simple in his personal tastes, and his indoor servants at Baskerville Hall consisted of a married couple named Barrymore, the

husband acting as butler and the wife as housekeeper. Their evidence, corroborated by that of several friends, tends to show that Sir Charles's health has for some time been impaired, and points especially to some affliction of the heart, manifesting itself in changes of color, breathlessness, and acute attacks of nervous depression. Dr. James Mortimer, a friend and medical attendant of the deceased, has given evidence to the same effect."

No hounds yet, I grumbled to myself. This case, which had begun so promisingly—with sticks to gnaw on and visiting spaniels no less—had degenerated into nothing more than a boring lecture presented by a tepid Don. I closed my eyes and prayed for sleep, but Mortimer's drone bore through to the center of my brain and prevented me from sinking into the arms of Morpheus.

"The facts of the case are simple. Sir Charles Baskerville was in the habit every night before going to bed of walking down the famous yew alley of Baskerville Hall. That night he went out as usual for his nocturnal walk, in the course of which he was in the habit of smoking a cigar. He never returned.

"At twelve o'clock Barrymore, finding the hall door still open, became alarmed, and, lighting a lantern, went in search of his master. The day had been wet, and Sir Charles's footmarks were easily traced down the alley. No signs of violence were to be discovered upon Sir Charles's person, and though the doctor's evidence pointed to an almost incredible facial distortion—so great that Dr. Mortimer refused at first to believe that it was indeed his friend and patient who lay before him—it was explained that that is a symptom which is not unusual in cases of death from cardiac exhaustion.

"This explanation was borne out by the post-mortem examination, which showed long-standing organic disease, and the coroner's jury returned a verdict in accordance with the medical evidence.

"Had the prosaic finding of the coroner not finally put an end to the romantic stories which have been whispered in connection with the affair, it might have been difficult to find a tenant for Baskerville Hall.

It is understood that the next of kin is Mr. Henry Baskerville, if he be still alive, the son of Sir Charles Baskerville's younger brother. The young man when last heard of was in America, and inquiries are being instituted with a view to informing him of his good fortune."

Dr. Mortimer refolded his paper and replaced it in his pocket. "Those are the public facts, Mr. Holmes, in connection with the death of Sir Charles Baskerville."

"I must thank you," said Sherlock Holmes, "for calling my attention to a case which certainly presents some features of interest. This article, you say, contains all the public facts?"

"It does."

"Then let me have the private ones."

He leaned back, put his finger-tips together, and assumed his most impassive and judicial expression. Since he was finding the case of interest, I felt it was the least I could do—as his able partner—to feign interest as well. To that end, I turned my head toward Mortimer.

"In doing so," said Dr. Mortimer, who had begun to show signs of some strong emotion, "I am telling that which I have not confided to anyone. My motive for withholding it from the coroner's inquiry is that a man of science shrinks from placing himself in the public position of seeming to endorse a popular superstition. I thought that I was justified in telling rather less than I knew, since no practical good could result from it, but with you there is no reason why I should not be perfectly frank.

"Within the last few months, it had become increasingly plain to me that Sir Charles's nervous system was strained to the breaking point. He had taken this legend of the hound exceedingly to heart—so much so that, although he would walk on his own grounds, nothing would induce him to go out upon the moor at night."

Holmes raised an eyebrow at this last statement, the only visible sign of interest he had demonstrated since Mortimer began this new recitation. I attempted to mirror the facial gesture, but with little success, my eyebrows being well-hidden within my fur.

"Incredible as it may appear to you, Mr. Holmes," Mortimer continued, "he was honestly convinced that a dreadful fate over-hung his family. The idea of some ghastly presence constantly haunted him, and on more than one occasion he has asked me whether I had on my medical journeys at night ever seen any strange creature or heard the baying of a hound. The latter question he put to me several times, and always with a voice which vibrated with excitement.

"It was at my advice that Sir Charles was about to go to London. His heart was, I knew, affected, and the constant anxiety in which he lived, however imaginary the cause of it might be, was evidently having a serious effect upon his health. I thought that a few months among the distractions of town would send him back a new man. At the last instant came this terrible catastrophe.

"On the night of Sir Charles's death, Barrymore—the butler who made the discovery—sent Perkins the groom on horseback to me, and I was able to reach Baskerville Hall within an hour of the event. I checked and corroborated all the facts which were mentioned at the inquest. I followed the footsteps down the yew alley, I saw the spot at the moor-gate where he seemed to have waited, I noted that there were no other footsteps save those of Barrymore on the soft gravel, and finally I carefully examined the body, which had not been touched until my arrival."

Yes, yes, yes I thought impatiently. The dead body is interest-ing, I'm sure. But what of the hound that you mentioned? I looked toward Holmes to see if he were as annoyed as I, but he appeared to still be in rapt attention. His eyes were closed and his fingertips were still pressed together. It was his serious expression and I saw it on him only when in the midst of an important case.

"Sir Charles lay on his face, his arms out, his fingers dug into the ground, and his features convulsed with some strong emotion to such an extent that I could hardly have sworn to his identity.

There was certainly no physical injury of any kind. But one false statement was made by Barrymore at the inquest. He said that there were no traces upon the ground around the body. He did not observe any. But I did—some little distance off, but fresh and clear."

"Footprints?"

"Footprints."

"A man's or a woman's?"

Dr. Mortimer looked strangely at us for an instant, and his voice sank almost to a whisper as he answered.

"Mr. Holmes, they were the footprints of a gigantic hound!"

I nearly jumped up in sheer excitement. This case was, at long last, finally becoming noteworthy.

CHAPTER 3

*T*he footprints of a gigantic hound! I confess upon hearing these words, a shudder passed through me. There was a thrill in the doctor's voice which showed that he was himself deeply moved by that which he recounted. Holmes leaned forward in his excitement and his eyes had the hard, dry glitter which they took on when he was keenly interested.

"You saw this?"

"As clearly as I see you."

"And you said nothing?"

"What was the use?"

"How was it that no one else saw it?"

"The marks were some twenty feet from the body and no one gave them a thought. I don't suppose I should have done so had I not known this legend."

My first thought turned to sheep-dogs, but the same had already occurred to Holmes. Our minds often ran in sync like that.

"There are many sheep-dogs on the moor?" asked Holmes.

"No doubt, but this was no sheep-dog."

"You say it was large?"

"Enormous."

"But it had not approached the body?"

"No."

I was up and alert, seated on my haunches. I looked to my right to see that Watson was also leaning forward as the conversation volleyed before us. Through a quick exchange of questions and answers, we quickly learned that the night was damp and raw, although not actually raining.

Holmes then went on to question Mortimer on the specifics of the location, with questions that absolutely paralleled the same line of inquiry I would have pursued.

We learned that there are two lines of old yew hedge, twelve feet high and impenetrable. The walk in the center was about eight feet across. Between the hedges and the walk there was a strip of grass about six feet broad on either side.

"I understand that the yew hedge is penetrated at one point by a gate?" said Holmes. He was still leaning forward and I discovered I was doing the same, unconsciously mirroring his posture.

"Yes, the wicket-gate which leads on to the moor," said Mortimer.

"Is there any other opening?"

"None."

"So that to reach the yew alley, one either has to come down it from the house or else to enter it by the moor-gate?"

"There is an exit through a summer-house at the far end."

"Had Sir Charles reached this?"

"No; he lay about fifty yards from it."

"Now, tell me, Dr. Mortimer—and this is important—the marks which you saw were on the path and not on the grass?"

This was a key point, as I knew it was unlikely footprints would be visible on the grass.

Mortimer shook his head. "No marks could show on the grass."

"Were they on the same side of the path as the moor-gate?"

"Yes; they were on the edge of the path on the same side as the moor-gate."

"This interests me exceedingly. Another point. Was the wicket-gate closed?"

"Closed and padlocked."

"How high was it?"

"About four feet high."

"Then anyone could have got over it?"

"Yes."

"And what marks did you see by the wicket-gate?"

"None in particular."

"Good heavens! Did no one examine it?"

"Yes, I examined it, myself."

"And found nothing?"

"It was all very confused. Sir Charles had evidently stood there for five or ten minutes."

"How do you know that?"

"Because the ash had twice dropped from his cigar."

"Excellent! This is a colleague, after our own heart." He looked in my direction upon making this statement, but I fear Dr. Watson misunderstood, thinking it was meant for him. I shook my head. Silly old fellow.

"But the marks?" continued Holmes.

"He had left his own marks all over that small patch of gravel. I could discern no others."

Sherlock Holmes struck his hand against his knee with an impatient gesture I had seen many times before.

"If I had only been there!" he cried.

I felt exactly the same as Holmes. This was evidently a case of extraordinary interest, and one which presented immense opportunities to scientific experts such as Sherlock and myself. Sadly, the gravel page upon which we might have read so much had since been smudged by the rain and defaced by the clogs of curious peasants. Those clues are long lost to us.

"Oh, Dr. Mortimer," continued Holmes. "Dr. Mortimer, to think that you should not have called me in! You have indeed much to answer for."

"I could not call you in, Mr. Holmes, without disclosing these facts to the world, and I have already given my reasons for not wishing to do so. Besides, besides—"

"Why do you hesitate?"

"There is a realm in which the most acute and most experienced of detectives is helpless."

"You mean that the thing is supernatural?"

"I did not positively say so."

No, he did not say it, but it was clear to me—and no doubt, to Holmes—that he evidently thought it.

"Since the tragedy, Mr. Holmes, there have come to my ears several incidents which are hard to reconcile with the settled order of Nature."

"For example?"

He then went on to explain that before the terrible event occurred, several people had seen a creature upon the moor. The beast corresponded with this Baskerville hound—the word he used was "demon"—and which, to his mind, could not possibly be any animal known to science.

All the witnesses agreed that it was a huge creature, luminous, ghastly, and spectral. They all told the same story of this dreadful apparition, exactly corresponding to the hell-hound of the legend.

"I assure you," Mortimer concluded, "that there is a reign of terror in the district, and that it is a hardy man who will cross the moor at night."

"And you, a trained man of science, believe it to be supernatural?"

"I do not know what to believe."

Holmes shrugged his shoulders, a shadow crossing his face. I think I understood his disquiet.

We have hitherto confined our investigations to this world. In a modest way, Holmes and I have combated evil, but to take on the Father of Evil himself would, perhaps, be too ambitious a task. I felt this in my heart and was certain Holmes shared my sentiment.

"I do not know what to believe," repeated Mortimer, more softly this time. "But I do know the original hound was material enough to tug a man's throat out, and yet he was diabolical as well."

"If you hold these views, why have you come to consult me at all? You tell me in the same breath that it is useless to investigate Sir Charles's death, and that you desire me to do it."

"I did not say that I desired you to do it."

"Then, how can I assist you?"

"By advising me as to what I should do with Sir Henry Baskerville, who arrives at Waterloo Station"—Dr. Mortimer looked at his watch—"in exactly one hour and a quarter."

"He being the heir?"

"Yes. On the death of Sir Charles we inquired for this young gentleman and found that he had been farming in Canada."

"There is no other claimant, I presume?"

"None. The only other kinsman whom we have been able to trace was Rodger Baskerville, the youngest of three brothers of whom poor Sir Charles was the elder. The second brother, who died young, is the father of this lad Henry. The third, Rodger, was the black sheep of the family. He made England too hot to hold him, fled to Central America, and died there in 1876 of yellow fever."

"So Henry is the last of the Baskervilles," Watson said, once again stating the obvious, which is—I believe—his most consistent contribution to our small band.

"Yes," Mortimer said. "And in one hour and five minutes I meet him at Waterloo Station. Now, Mr. Holmes, what would you advise me to do with him?"

"Why should he not go to the home of his fathers?"

"It seems natural, does it not? And yet, consider that every Baskerville who goes there meets with an evil fate. And yet it cannot be denied that the prosperity of the whole poor, bleak countryside depends upon his presence. All the good work which has been done by Sir Charles will crash to the ground if there is no tenant of the Hall."

Holmes considered for a little time.

"Put into plain words, the matter is this," said he. "In your opinion there is a diabolical agency which makes Dartmoor an unsafe abode for a Baskerville—that is your opinion?"

"At least I might go the length of saying that there is some evidence that this may be so."

"Exactly. But surely, if your supernatural theory be correct, it could do the young man evil in London as easily as in Devonshire. A devil with merely local powers like a parish vestry would be too inconceivable a thing."

"Your advice, then, as I understand it, is that the young man will be as safe in Devonshire as in London. He comes in fifty minutes. What would you recommend?"

"I recommend, sir, that you take a cab and proceed to Waterloo to meet Sir Henry Baskerville."

"And then?"

"And then you will say nothing to him at all until I have made up my mind about the matter."

"How long will it take you to make up your mind?"

"Twenty-four hours. At ten o'clock tomorrow, Dr. Mortimer, I will be much obliged to you if you will call upon me here. And it will be of help to me in my plans for the future if you will bring Sir Henry Baskerville with you."

"I will do so, Mr. Holmes." He headed toward the door in his strange, peering, absent-minded fashion, his spaniel directly on his heels. Holmes stopped him at the head of the stair.

"Only one more question, Dr. Mortimer. You say that before

Sir Charles Baskerville's death several people saw this apparition upon the moor?"

"Three people did."

"Did any see it after?"

"I have not heard of any."

"Thank you. Good-morning."

Holmes returned to his seat with that quiet look of inward satisfaction which meant that we had a congenial task before us. He settled back into his settee and I positioned myself back upon my hearth-rug. Watson, recognizing there was little he could add to our upcoming cerebral session, stood up and gathered his coat.

"Going out, Watson?"

"Unless I can help you in some manner?"

"When you pass Bradley's, would you ask him to send up a pound of his strongest shag tobacco? Thank you. It would be as well if you could make it convenient not to return before evening. Then I should be very glad to compare impressions as to this most interesting problem which has been submitted to us this morning."

* * *

I KNEW THAT SECLUSION AND SOLITUDE WERE THE VERY SOUL OF necessity for my master and myself in these hours of shared intense mental concentration. During this time together, we weighed every particle of evidence, constructed alternative theories, balanced one against the other, and made up our minds as to which points were essential and which immaterial. These times were always my favorite with Holmes. No words needed to be spoken, just a quiet air of intense concentration on his part and the occasional nap on mine.

That was how we spent our afternoon and it was well into evening when I heard Dr. Watson's familiar steps on the stairs.

My guess is that his first impression as he opened the door was that a fire had broken out, for the room was so filled with smoke that the light of the lamp upon the table was blurred by it. As he entered, however, his fears were set at rest, for it was the acrid fumes of strong coarse tobacco which took him by the throat and set him coughing.

Although I enjoyed the smoky environment less than he did, I had—over the course of these long afternoons—become accustomed to it. Through the haze from my position on the hearth-rug, I had a vague vision of Holmes in his dressing-gown coiled up in an armchair with his black clay pipe between his lips. Several rolls of paper lay around him. He looked up at the sound of Watson's reflexive coughing attack.

"Caught cold, Watson?" said he.

"No, it's this poisonous atmosphere."

"I suppose it is pretty thick, now that you mention it."

"Thick! It is intolerable."

"Open the window, then!"

Watson moved toward the window, grumbling as he did. I got a good look at him as he passed and recognized immediately that he had spent the majority of the last few hours at his club. Holmes must have come to a similar conclusion, for at that moment he uttered the same thought aloud.

"You have been at your club all day, I perceive," said Holmes.

"My dear Holmes!"

"Am I right?"

"Certainly, but how?"

He laughed at Watson's bewildered expression and glanced toward me, recognizing we had both come to the same conclusion.

"Septimus and I both recognized it, the moment you walked in. A gentleman goes forth on a showery and miry day. He returns immaculate in the evening with the gloss still on his hat and his boots. He has been a fixture therefore all day. He is not a man with intimate friends. Where, then, could he have been? Is it not obvious?"

It was, in fact quite obvious, but Watson seemed to take no pleasure at our revelation.

"Where do you think that I have been?" asked Holmes.

"A fixture also," Watson grumbled as he settled into his chair. "Like the dog here, spread out and unmoving for the whole of the afternoon."

"On that you are mistaken. Mrs. Hudson stopped up once. Or twice, I forget. To take Septimus out."

It had been twice during the course of the afternoon and early evening, and after the second trip, she had been kind enough to fill my bowl with kibble and check on the contents of my water bowl, which were arid to the extreme.

I have learned that there are many benefits to living with a mind as keen as Sherlock Holmes', but regular outings and a consistent meal schedule are not among them.

"On the contrary, I have been quite active. I have been to Devonshire," said Holmes.

"In spirit?"

"Well, yes, exactly. My body has remained in this apartment."

That was true, to a point. He had also consumed two large pots of coffee and an incredible amount of tobacco. In addition, he had sent down to Stamford's for the Ordnance map of that portion of the moor, and the two of us had hovered over it all day. After hours of study, I flatter myself that I could find my way about, simply on the basis of the time I'd spent watching him pour over the map.

"I traveled there with this."

He unrolled one section of the large map and held it over his knee. "Here you have the particular district which concerns us. That is Baskerville Hall in the middle."

"With a wood round it?"

"Exactly."

With that, Holmes launched into a quick tour for Watson's benefit of the areas he and I had covered in such detail that afternoon.

He pointed to a small clump of buildings which represented the hamlet of Grimpen, where Dr. Mortimer and his spaniel made their home. Around it were very few scattered dwellings, such as Lafter Hall and a house which may be the residence of the naturalist—Stapleton, if I remember right, was the name which Holmes uttered.

He pointed out two moorland farmhouses, High Tor and Foulmire, and then indicated—fourteen miles away, but a mere matter of inches with his long, boney finger—the great convict prison of Princetown. Between and around these scattered points extended the desolate, lifeless moor.

This, then, was the stage upon which tragedy has been played, and upon which, I hoped, we may help to solve the devilish mystery.

"Tell me Holmes," asked Dr. Watson at the conclusion of this brief, cartographical tour, "Are you yourself inclining to the supernatural explanation?"

Holmes considered the question for a long moment.

"If Dr. Mortimer's surmise should be correct, and we are dealing with forces outside the ordinary laws of Nature," began Holmes, "there is an end of our investigation. But we are bound to exhaust all other hypotheses before falling back upon this one. I think we'll shut that window again, if you don't mind. It is a singular thing, but I find that a concentrated atmosphere helps a concentration of thought."

Holmes stood up and closed the window, bringing to a halt the small stream of fresh air which had begun to make its way into our smoky rooms.

"Have you turned the case over in your mind?" he asked as he returned to his chair.

"Yes, I have thought a good deal of it in the course of the day."

"What do you make of it?"

"It is very bewildering."

"It has certainly a character of its own. There are points of distinction about it. That change in the footprints, for example. What do you make of that?"

The two men went on at some length about that point, which to my mind was simplicity itself. Some fool at the inquest had said it looked as if Baskerville had walked on tiptoe down a portion of the alley. If anyone had every observed my own footprints, as I transitioned from a mere canter into a full run, they might have come to the same false conclusion. My fastest running gait, a double suspension rotary gallop, puts all four of my feet free from the ground during each full stride, in two distinct phases, contracted and extended.

It was clear in my mind that the footprints indicated that Baskerville had been running—running desperately, running for his life, running until he burst his heart—and fell dead upon his face.

That of course raised the question of what was it he was running from? The only answer, to my mind, was that he must have lost his wits. Only a man who had lost his wits would have run *from* the house instead of *towards* it. I can't imagine a dog making the same rash decision.

"So you think that he was waiting for someone?"

Watson's question to Holmes pulled me back into their conversation.

"The man was elderly and infirm," Holmes was saying. "We can understand his taking an evening stroll, but the ground was damp and the night inclement. Is it natural that he should stand for five or ten minutes, as Dr. Mortimer has suggested and deduced from the cigar ash?"

"But he went out every evening."

"True, but I think it unlikely that he waited at the moor-gate every evening. On the contrary, the evidence is that he avoided the moor. That night he waited there. The thing takes shape, Watson. It becomes coherent."

On this point, I had to agree with Holmes. The story was taking shape in my mind. What I needed was time to consider all the factors in more depth. For me, my best thinking often occurs just as I'm falling asleep or in those first few moments upon awakening. I made my way to the worn spot on the hearth-rug which I call my own and settled in to consider the matter. Holmes, it appeared, was in a similar state.

"Might I ask you to hand me my violin," I heard him say to Watson, "and we will postpone all further thought upon this business until we have had the advantage of meeting Dr. Mortimer and Sir Henry Baskerville in the morning."

With that, he began to play and I, mercifully, began to sleep.

CHAPTER 4

*O*ur clients were punctual to their appointment, for the clock had just struck ten when Dr. Mortimer was shown up, followed by the young baronet. The latter was a small, alert, dark-eyed man about thirty years of age, very sturdily built, with thick black eyebrows and a strong, pugnacious face.

He wore a ruddy-tinted tweed suit and had the weather-beaten appearance of one who has spent most of his time in the open air. Yet there was something in his steady eye and the quiet assurance of his bearing which indicated the gentleman. At another time, in another life, he might have made a fine greyhound.

The most notable thing about their arrival, I noted sadly, was the distinct lack of a spaniel among their company. While Holmes ushered the two men in, I made a cursory check of the small vestibule outside our door, on the off chance the dog was lagging behind. This was not the case. A quick glimpse down the stairs at the front door confirmed this situation.

"This is Sir Henry Baskerville," Dr. Mortimer was saying as I returned to the room. The introduction seemed to me unnecessary;

alas, who else could it have been? That was whom he had promised to bring. There were handshakes all around, so I took the opportunity to visit my water dish before the proceedings commenced.

"The strange thing is," said Baskerville, "that if my friend here had not proposed coming round to you this morning, I should have come on my own account. I understand that you think out little puzzles, and I've had one this morning which wants more thinking out than I am able to give it."

"Pray take a seat, Sir Henry," said Holmes, gesturing to the settee. I took my position on the hearth-rug while the humans settled themselves in. "Do I understand you to say that you have yourself had some remarkable experience since you arrived in London?

"Nothing of much importance, Mr. Holmes. Only a joke, as like as not. It was this letter, if you can call it a letter, which reached me this morning."

He laid an envelope upon the table, and they all bent over it. From where I lay, I could see it was of common quality, grayish in color.

Holmes looked at the envelope for a long moment.

"The address, 'Sir Henry Baskerville, Northumberland Hotel,' has been printed in rough characters. The post-mark is 'Charing Cross,' and the date of posting is last evening," he reported. He turned, glancing keenly across at our visitor. "Who knew that you were going to the Northumberland Hotel?"

"No one could have known. We only decided after I met Dr. Mortimer."

"But Dr. Mortimer was no doubt already stopping there?"

"No, I had been staying with a friend," said the doctor.

"There was no possible indication that we intended to go to this hotel," said Baskerville.

"Hum! Someone seems to be very deeply interested in your movements."

Out of the envelope he took a half-sheet of paper folded into four. This he opened and spread flat upon the table.

"Interesting," he said slowly. "Across the middle of the sheet a single sentence has been formed by the expedient of pasting printed words upon it. It reads: 'As you value your life or your reason, keep away from the moor.'"

"And yet," he continued, "the word 'moor' is the only one in the sentence printed in ink. Have you yesterday's Times, Watson?"

"It is here in the corner."

"Might I trouble you for it—the inside page, please, with the leading articles?" He took the paper and glanced swiftly over it, running his eyes up and down the columns. "Capital article here on free trade. I won't bore you by reading it, but I will point out that it contains, among many others, the following words: 'You,' 'your,' 'your,' 'life,' 'reason,' 'value,' 'keep away,' and 'from the.' Don't you see now whence these words have been taken?"

He held up the letter alongside the newspaper in order to reinforce his point.

"By thunder, you're right! Well, if that isn't smart!" cried Sir Henry.

"If any possible doubt remained, it is settled by the fact that 'keep away' and 'from the' are cut out in one piece."

"Well, now—so it is!"

"Really, Mr. Holmes, I could understand anyone saying that the words were from a newspaper," said Dr. Mortimer, gazing at my master in amazement. "But that you should name which, and add that it came from the leading article, is really one of the most remarkable things which I have ever known. How did you do it?"

"Because a Times leader is entirely distinctive, and these words could have been taken from nothing else. As it was done yesterday, the strong probability was that we should find the words in yesterday's issue."

"So far as I can follow you, then, Mr. Holmes," said Sir Henry Baskerville, "someone cut out this message with a scissors—"

"Nail-scissors," said Holmes. "You can see that it was a very short-bladed scissors, since the cutter had to take two snips to cut out 'keep away.'"

"That is so. Someone, then, cut out the message with a pair of short-bladed scissors, pasted it with paste—"

"Gum," said Holmes.

"With gum on to the paper. But I want to know why the word 'moor' should have been written?"

"Because he could not find it in print. The other words were all simple and might be found in any issue, but 'moor' would be less common."

"Why, of course, that would explain it. Have you read anything else in this message, Mr. Holmes?"

"The Times is a paper which is seldom found in any hands but those of the highly educated. We may take it, therefore, that the letter was composed by an educated man who wished to pose as an uneducated one, and his effort to conceal his own writing suggests that that writing might be known, or come to be known, by you. Now, you might call it a guess, no doubt, but I am almost certain that this address on the envelope has been written in a hotel."

"How in the world can you say that?"

"If you examine it carefully you will see that both the pen and the ink have given the writer trouble."

He held the envelope and the sheet of paper up for the group and for the first time I cast my eyes upon them. I agreed immediately with Holmes' assessment that the type had come from a copy of the Times. In my youth, my kennel had been feathered with several of the best London papers—shredded but still legible—and I learned early on to tell at a glance the differences between them.

I also agreed with his thinking that the author had struggled with both the pen and the ink. I could easily recognize, even from my position across the room—I am, after all, a sight hound—that the pen had spluttered twice in a single word and had run dry three times in the short address. This, I felt, demonstrated that there had been very little ink in the bottle.

I've observed both Holmes and Dr. Watson in the act of writing on numerous occasions, and recognized a private pen or ink-bottle would seldom be allowed to be in such a state, and the combination of the two must be quite rare.

But having traveled with Holmes on numerous occasions and listened to his loud, vocal displeasure at the untidy state of hotel pens and hotel ink, I think it was safe to surmise that the letter was written in a hotel. And it appeared that Holmes agreed with me on this point.

"Yes," he was saying to the small group, "I have very little hesitation in saying that could we examine the waste-paper baskets of the hotels around Charing Cross until we found the remains of the mutilated Times leader, we could lay our hands straight upon the person who sent this singular message."

He set the letter and envelope back down on the table and turned to our guests.

"And now, Sir Henry, has anything else of interest happened to you since you have been in London?"

"Well, it depends upon what you think worth reporting."

"I think anything out of the ordinary routine of life well worth reporting."

Sir Henry smiled. "I don't know much of British life yet, for I have spent nearly all my time in the States and in Canada. But I hope that to lose one of your boots is not part of the ordinary routine of life over here."

"You have lost one of your boots?"

My ears perked up at this new information and I felt a sudden wave of unfounded guilt. In my youth I had—on more than one occasion, I am sad to report—been justly accused of stealing a boot or a shoe, for the simple gnawing pleasure it might provide. I am happy to report I have long since outgrown this anti-social behavior. Yet the shame of my youthful actions haunt me still.

I scanned their faces to see if there was to be a dramatic *j'accuse!* moment in my near future. However, none of them were paying me the least attention. And for once, I was grateful to be ignored.

"Well, mislaid it, anyhow," continued Sir Henry. "I put them both outside my door last night, and there was only one in the morning. I could get no sense out of the chap who cleans them. The worst of it is that I only bought the pair last night in the Strand, and I have never had them on."

"If you have never worn them, why did you put them out to be cleaned?"

"They were tan boots and had never been varnished."

"It seems a singularly useless thing to steal," said Dr. Watson.

"And, now, gentlemen," said the baronet with decision, "it seems to me that I have spoken quite enough about the little that I know. It is time that you kept your promise and gave me a full account of what we are all driving at."

"Your request is a very reasonable one," answered Holmes. "Dr. Mortimer, I think you could not do better than to tell your story as you told it to us."

Thus encouraged, the young doctor drew his papers from his pocket and presented the whole case. Sir Henry Baskerville listened with the deepest attention and with an occasional exclamation of surprise. For my part, I napped during most of it, having heard it well enough the morning before.

"I seem to have come into an inheritance with a vengeance," said Sir Henry when the long narrative was finished. "Of course, I've heard of the hound ever since I was in the nursery. It's the pet story of the family, though I never thought of taking it seriously before. But as to my uncle's death—you don't seem quite to have made up your mind whether it's a case for a policeman or a clergyman."

"Precisely."

"And now there's this affair of the letter to me at the hotel. I suppose that fits into its place."

"It seems to show that someone knows more than we do about what goes on upon the moor," said Dr. Mortimer.

"And also," said Holmes, "that someone is not ill-disposed towards you, since they warn you of danger."

"Or it may be that they wish, for their own purposes, to scare me away."

"Well, of course, that is possible also. I am very much indebted to you, Dr. Mortimer, for introducing me to a problem which presents several interesting alternatives. But the practical point which we now have to decide, Sir Henry, is whether it is or is not advisable for you to go to Baskerville Hall."

"Why should I not go?"

"There seems to be danger."

"Do you mean danger from this family fiend or do you mean danger from human beings?"

"Well, that is what we have to find out."

"Whichever it is, my answer is fixed. There is no devil in hell, Mr. Holmes, and there is no man upon earth who can prevent me from going to the home of my own people, and you may take that to be my final answer."

His dark brows knitted and his face flushed to a dusky red as he spoke. It was evident that the fiery temper of the Baskervilles was not extinct in this, their last representative.

"Meanwhile," said he, "I have hardly had time to think over all that you have told me. I should like to have a quiet hour by myself to make up my mind. It's half-past eleven now and I am going back right away to my hotel. Suppose you and your friend, Dr. Watson, come round and lunch with us at two. I'll be able to tell you more clearly then how this thing strikes me."

"Is that convenient to you, Watson?"

"Perfectly."

"Then you may expect us. Shall I have a cab called?"

"I'd prefer to walk, for this affair has flurried me rather."

"I'll join you in a walk, with pleasure," said his companion.

"Then we meet again at two o'clock. Au revoir, and good-morning!"

* * *

WE HEARD THE STEPS OF OUR VISITORS DESCEND THE STAIR AND THE bang of the front door. In an instant, Holmes had changed from the languid dreamer to the man of action.

"Your hat and boots, Watson, quick! And take down Septimus' leash, if you please. Not a moment to lose!" He rushed into his room in his dressing-gown and was back again in a few seconds in a frock-coat. With my leash quickly secured, we hurried together down the stairs and into the street.

Dr. Mortimer and Baskerville were still visible about two hundred yards ahead of us in the direction of Oxford Street.

"Shall I run on and stop them?" asked Watson.

I looked up at Holmes, who knew—when it came to running—I would be the smarter choice. He shook his head at both of us.

"Not for the world. I am perfectly satisfied with the company of my friend and my dog, if you will tolerate mine. Dr. Mortimer and Baskerville are wise, for it is certainly a very fine morning for a walk."

He quickened his pace until we had decreased the distance which divided us by about half. Then, still keeping a hundred yards behind, we followed them into Oxford Street and so down Regent Street.

At one point the two gentlemen stopped and stared into a shop window, upon which Holmes, Watson and I did the same. An instant afterwards he gave a little cry of satisfaction, and, following the direction of his eager eyes, I saw that a hansom cab with a man inside, which had halted on the other side of the street, was now proceeding slowly onward again.

"There's our man! Come along! We'll have a good look at him, if we can do no more."

At that instant I was aware of a bushy black beard and a pair of piercing eyes turned upon us through the side window of the cab. Instantly the trapdoor at the top flew up, something was screamed to the driver, and the cab flew madly off down Regent Street. Holmes looked eagerly round for another, but no empty cab was in sight. Then he dashed in wild pursuit amid the stream of the traffic, but the start was too great, and already the cab was out of sight.

I pulled sharply on my leash, but he looked down at me and offered me a quick shake of his head. "No, I have no doubt you would run them to ground, Septimus," he said quietly. "But not in London traffic. Too many ways for a keen racer such as yourself to be injured, I'm afraid. Were we in the country…"

There was no need for him to complete the thought. We both knew that in an open field, without the hazards of an urban traffic pattern, I would have been unstoppable. He patted my head warmly and tugged on my leash, pulling me closer to him.

"Well, it was evident from what we have seen and heard that Baskerville has been very closely shadowed by someone since he has been in town. How else could it be known so quickly that it was the Northumberland Hotel which he had chosen? If they had followed him the first day I argued that they would follow him also the second. And, clearly, I have been proven correct on that presumption."

"What a pity we did not get the number of the cab!"

Holmes and I exchanged a quick look, for we had both separately spotted the number and immediately committed it to memory.

"My dear Watson, clumsy as I have been, you surely do not seriously imagine that I neglected to get the number? No. 2704 is our man."

We had been sauntering slowly down Regent Street during

this conversation. Dr. Mortimer and his companion had long vanished in front of us.

"There is no object in our following them," said Holmes. "The shadow has departed and will not return. We must see what further cards we have in our hands and play them with precision. Could you swear to that man's face within the cab?"

"I could swear only to the beard."

"And so could I—from which I gather that, in all probability, it was a false one."

From the quick look I had gotten, I was sure it was undoubtedly false. I was even able to spot the small hooks which hung it upon the man's slightly oversized ears. I smiled, not for the first time, at the greatly limited eyesight of my human companions. How they made it through a day without serious injury to their persons was beyond me.

Holmes turned suddenly into one of the district messenger offices and I followed right behind him. Watson, who was taken by surprise by this sudden shift in direction, followed a few addled steps behind us.

Once in the messenger office, we were warmly greeted by the manager.

"Ah, Mr. Holmes and his handsome assistant," the manager said. "Can I offer him a treat?"

"By all means," Holmes agreed and a moment later I was crunching on a meaty-tasting baked good that, for some unknown reason, had been fashioned into the shape of a bone.

"So, Wilson, I see you have not forgotten the little case in which I had the good fortune to help you?" said Holmes.

"No, sir, indeed I have not. You and Septimus there saved my good name, and perhaps my life."

"My dear fellow, you exaggerate. I have some recollection, Wilson, that you had among your boys a lad named Cartwright, who showed some ability during the investigation."

"Yes, sir, he is still with us."

"Could you ring him up? — thank you! And I should be glad to have change of this five-pound note."

Before changing the bill, Mr. Wilson was kind enough to extend to me yet another of his bone-shaped treats, which I accepted with warm gratitude.

A few moments later, a lad of fourteen, with a bright, keen face, appeared in the office. He gave me a friendly pat on the head and then stood there gazing with great reverence at the famous detective. Sadly, he showed no interest whatsoever in Dr. Watson, who seemed a trifle miffed at being the odd man out in this scenario.

"Let me have the Hotel Directory," said Holmes to Mr. Wilson. "Thank you! Now, Cartwright, there are the names of twenty-three hotels here, all in the immediate neighborhood of Charing Cross. Do you see?"

"Yes, sir."

"You will visit each of these in turn."

"Yes, sir."

"You will begin in each case by giving the outside porter one shilling. Here are twenty-three shillings."

"Yes, sir."

"You will tell him that you want to see the waste-paper of yesterday. You will say that an important telegram has miscarried and that you are looking for it. You understand?"

"Yes, sir."

"But what you are really looking for is the center page of the Times with some holes cut in it with scissors. Here is a copy of the Times. It is this page. You could easily recognize it, could you not?"

"Yes, sir."

"In each case the outside porter will send for the hall porter, to whom also you will give a shilling. Here are twenty-three more shillings."

Holmes handed the boy the second set of coins; he assiduously put one set in his right pocket and the other set in his left.

"You will then learn in possibly twenty cases out of the twenty-three that the waste of the day before has been burned or removed," continued Holmes. "In the three other cases you will be shown a heap of paper and you will look for this page of the Times among it. The odds are enormously against your finding it."

"I'll do my best, sir," said Cartwright. He glanced down at me and then grabbed another treat for me from behind the counter. He was a fine boy.

Holmes held out another, smaller set of coins. "There are ten shillings extra in case of emergencies. Let me have a report by wire at Baker Street before evening and there will be a quid in it for you."

With that last bit of incentive, Cartwright flew out of the office, intent upon the task before him. Holmes watched him go then turned to Dr. Watson, who had observed the exchange closely. For myself, my attention was on the cubby behind the counter which held the treats and what it might take to gain access to it.

"And now, Watson, it only remains for us to find out by wire the identity of the cabman, No. 2704," said Holmes. "And then, since it is still such a fine day, we'll give Septimus here a much-needed walk and fill in the time until we are due at the hotel."

CHAPTER 5

*T*he walk, while far too brief in duration, was delightfully instructive, from my point of view at least.

Some perspective is required. Walks engineered by Holmes' landlady, Mrs. Hudson, tended to be focused affairs, with a set start time, an end time and a clear route and well-determined final destination. She was not one for a rambling stroll or for frequent stops to investigate this odor or that paw print. She was, in a word, focused. In addition, her walks were filled with a seemingly-endless stream of directions issuing forth, including "Come along now," "Quick, do your business, that's a good boy," and "Let's head toward home, luv. Mama's getting tired."

In stark contrast, a walk led by Sherlock Holmes was, generally, a shambling affair. He often had no destination in mind, certainly possessed no sense of time, and was impervious to any sort of weather, from blistering sun to pouring rain to the chilliest of London mornings. In short, he was an ideal guide, often so lost in his own thoughts that we'd as likely end up in Shepherd's Bush or Belgravia if not for my innate sense of direction to guide us safely home.

That afternoon's short walk with Holmes and Watson afforded me some rare time to build on my base of knowledge on footprints (squirrel versus rabbit versus chipmunk) as well as to explore, via my less-than-ideal olfactory system, some delightful and instructive new odors found near the base of a yew tree. I could have spent an hour or more on that sapling alone, but before I knew it, time was up and we found ourselves at the Northumberland Hotel.

"Sir Henry Baskerville is upstairs expecting you," said the clerk. "He asked me to show you up at once when you came." He glanced down and saw me, standing alongside my master, leaning protectively against his leg. It looked as if the clerk were about to comment on my presence, but Holmes spoke first.

"Excellent," said Holmes. "We have secured the greyhound Sir Henry requested. I am assuming we should bring that up with us as well?"

The clerk nodded without conviction. "Yes, I believe so, yes," he stammered, again looking down in my direction.

"Brilliant, as it was quite difficult to locate a hound with the specifications he had insisted upon."

"Was it?"

"It was," said Holmes, with a tone which more than suggested this area of conversation was now completed. "But while I have your attention, do you have any objection to my looking at your register? On Sir Henry's behalf?"

The clerk, flummoxed by the sudden change in topic, immediately acquiesced. "Not in the least." He spun the large volume around for Holmes' examination.

"See here, Watson," said Holmes. "The register shows that two names had been added after that of Baskerville. One was Theophilus Johnson and family, of Newcastle; the other Mrs. Oldmore and maid, of High Lodge, Alton."

Holmes looked up at the clerk.

"Surely that must be the same Johnson whom I used to know,"

said Holmes. "A lawyer, is he not, gray-headed, and walks with a limp?"

"No, sir, this is Mr. Johnson, the coal-owner, a very active gentleman, not older than yourself."

"Surely you are mistaken about his trade?"

"No, sir! he has used this hotel for many years, and he is very well known to us."

"Ah, that settles it. Mrs. Oldmore, too; I seem to remember the name. Excuse my curiosity, but often in calling upon one friend one finds another."

"She is an invalid lady, sir. Her husband was once mayor of Gloucester. She always comes to us when she is in town."

"Thank you; I am afraid I must admit I cannot claim her acquaintance."

We headed away from the desk toward the main stairway.

"We have established a most important fact by these questions," continued Holmes in a low voice as the three of us climbed the stairs together. "We know now that the people who are so interested in our friend have not settled down in his own hotel. That means that while they are, as we have seen, very anxious to watch him, they are equally anxious that he should not see them. Now, this is a most suggestive fact."

"What does it suggest?"

"It suggests—halloa, my dear fellow, what on earth is the matter?"

As we came round the top of the stairs, we ran up against Sir Henry Baskerville himself. His face was flushed with anger, and he held an old and dusty boot in one of his hands. Right behind him, looking dazed, was Dr. Mortimer. Sadly, he appeared to be sans spaniel.

"Seems to me they are playing me for a sucker in this hotel," cried Sir Henry. "They'll find they've started in to monkey with the wrong man unless they are careful. By thunder, if that chap can't find my missing boot there will be trouble."

"Still looking for your boot?"

"Yes, sir, and I mean to find it."

"But, surely, you said that it was a new brown boot?"

"So it was, sir. And now it's an old black one."

"What! you don't mean to say?"

"That's just what I do mean to say," said Sir Henry. "I only had three pairs in the world—the new brown, the old black, and the patent leathers, which as you can see I am wearing. Yesterday they took one of my new brown ones, and today they have sneaked one of the black. Well, have you got it? Speak out, man, and don't stand staring!"

An agitated German waiter had appeared upon the scene.

"No, sir; I have made inquiry all over the hotel, but I can hear no word of it."

"Well, either that boot comes back before sundown or I'll see the manager and tell him that I intend to go straight out of this hotel."

"It shall be found, sir—I promise you that if you will have a little patience it will be found," said the old waiter as he scuttled away.

"Mind it is, for it's the last thing of mine that I'll lose in this den of thieves," said Sir Henry. He took a breath and appeared to calm, if only to a small degree. He turned and we followed him into his sitting room, where he gestured the men to several over-stuffed chairs.

While they took their seats, I turned my attention to the boot. Holmes had dropped my leash and so I made my way across the richly-appointed room, while the humans busied themselves in the odd human custom of waiting for one another to sit. Sir Henry had tossed the offending boot on the floor, where it lay next to a lone brand-new boot. This, I surmised, must be the remaining one from the pair he had spoken of this morning.

I inspected the mis-matched set with interest as I vaguely listened to Sir Henry and Holmes focus on more prosaic issues.

"Well, well, Mr. Holmes, you'll excuse my troubling you about such a trifle—" said Sir Henry.

"On the whole," said Holmes as he settled into a chair, "I think that your decision is a wise one. While I don't see an immediate connection to this boot affair, I have ample evidence that you are being followed in London."

I studied the two boots closely: One, evidently new and unworn offered very little aromatic history; the other, weathered and timeworn, presented a virtual panoply of history emanating from it.

While I have some small experience in the art of detecting via my sense of smell, I do not, for one moment, compare my olfactory skills to those of Toby, a bloodhound Holmes employs on occasion. While you may think our relationship might be a contentious or competitive one, that could not be further from the truth. We respect each other's unique skills and each looks upon the other as an expert in his respective field.

At this moment, and not for the first time, I wished I had the resources to contact Toby's owner, a Mr. Sherman at Number 3 Pinchin Lane in Lambeth, in order to arrange a short consultation with the brilliant brown and white mutt. I was sure Toby could easily and quickly deliver a richer and more finessed assessment of the mismatched brogans before me than I might generate on my own.

"You did not know, Dr. Mortimer" Holmes was saying, "that you were followed this morning from my house?"

Dr. Mortimer started violently. "Followed! By whom?"

"That, unfortunately, is what I cannot tell you. Have you among your neighbors or acquaintances on Dartmoor any man with a black, full beard?"

"No—or, let me see—why, yes. Barrymore, Sir Charles's butler, is a man with a full, black beard."

"Ha! Where is Barrymore?"

"He is in charge of the Hall."

"We had best ascertain if he is really there, or if by any possibility he might be in London."

Holmes then launched into a complicated plan—something about sending a telegram to Barrymore at Baskerville Hall, to determine if he was in fact there—which offered no interest to me whatsoever. I already knew that the fellow who had been tailing Dr. Mortimer and Sir Henry that morning had been wearing a false beard, so it was clear—to me, at least—he could not have been Barrymore.

While they proceeded with their plan, I narrowed my investigative focus to the older of the two boots before me. This was, I could immediately ascertain, a piece of footwear which had seen the world. While I recognized the streets of London on its outer sheen, beneath that layer were a multitude of stratum, each one offering a new smell sensation. And, on every layer, one smell stood-out: This boot had clearly belong to Sir Henry Baskerville for much if not all of its leathery life.

I looked up from my musings to discover Holmes pacing while he held court.

"We hold several threads in our hands, Sir Henry, and the odds are that one or other of them will guide us to the truth," said Holmes. "We may waste time in following the wrong one, but sooner or later we must come upon the right."

There was general agreement concerning this assessment—I concurred as well—but before more details could be elucidated, a hotel waiter entered to inform us that lunch was being served.

AFTER A PLEASANT LUNCHEON—WHICH, THOUGHTFULLY, INCLUDED a small dish of water and a scoop of pâté for myself on the floor near Holmes' place at table—we returned to the sitting room. Luncheon conversation had studiously avoided the case at hand, which I suspect was Holmes' scheme. He rarely enjoyed mixing dining with his work. Instead there was talk of local politics, the hunting near the Baskerville estate, and other subjects of which I took little note.

However, once we had repaired to the sitting room, Holmes asked Baskerville what might be his intentions.

"To go to Baskerville Hall," said Sir Henry.

"And when?"

"At the end of the week."

"Tell me, did Barrymore profit at all by Sir Charles's will?" asked Holmes as he turned to Dr. Mortimer.

"He and his wife had five hundred pounds each," said Mortimer.

"Ha! Did they know that they would receive this?"

"Yes; Sir Charles was very fond of talking about the provisions of his will."

"That is very interesting."

"I hope," said Dr. Mortimer, "that you do not look with suspicious eyes upon everyone who received a legacy from Sir Charles, for I also had a thousand pounds left to me."

"Indeed! And anyone else?"

"There were many insignificant sums to individuals, and a large number of public charities. The residue all went to Sir Henry."

"And how much was the residue?"

"Seven hundred and forty thousand pounds."

Holmes raised his eyebrows in surprise. "I had no idea that so gigantic a sum was involved," said he.

"Sir Charles had the reputation of being rich, but we did not know how very rich he was until we came to examine his securities. The total value of the estate was close on to a million."

"Dear me! It is a stake for which a man might well play a desperate game. And one more question, Dr. Mortimer. Supposing that anything happened to our young friend here—you will forgive the unpleasant hypothesis!—who would inherit the estate?"

"Since Rodger Baskerville, Sir Charles's younger brother died unmarried, the estate would descend to the Desmonds, who are distant cousins. James Desmond is an elderly clergyman in Westmoreland."

"Have you met Mr. James Desmond?"

"Yes; he once came down to visit Sir Charles. He is a man of venerable appearance and of saintly life. I remember that he refused to accept any settlement from Sir Charles, though he pressed it upon him."

"And this man of simple tastes would be the heir to Sir Charles's thousands?"

"He would be the heir to the estate because that is entailed. He would also be the heir to the money unless it were willed otherwise by the present owner, who can, of course, do what he likes with it."

"And have you made your will, Sir Henry?"

"No, Mr. Holmes, I have not. I've had no time, for it was only yesterday that I learned how matters stood. But in any case I feel that the money should go with the title and estate. That was my poor uncle's idea. How is the owner going to restore the glories of the Baskervilles if he has not money enough to keep up the property?"

"Quite so. Well, Sir Henry, I am of one mind with you as to the advisability of your going down to Devonshire without delay. There is only one provision which I must make. You certainly must not go alone."

"Dr. Mortimer returns with me."

"But Dr. Mortimer has his practice to attend to, and his house is miles away from yours. With all the goodwill in the world he may be unable to help you. No, Sir Henry, you must take with you someone who will be always by your side."

"Is it possible that you could come yourself, Mr. Holmes?"

"If matters came to a crisis I should endeavor to be present in person; but you can understand that, with my extensive consulting practice and with the constant appeals which reach me from many quarters, it is impossible for me to be absent from London for an indefinite time."

"Whom would you recommend, then?"

"I suggest you take Septimus," he began and then turned to Watson. "By which I mean, of course, that Watson and the dog should accompany you. If my friend would undertake it, there is no one who is better worth having at your side when you are in a tight place. No one can say so more confidently than I."

The proposition took me completely by surprise. I recognize the value I occasionally brought to our endeavors, but wasn't prepared for such a sudden outburst of enthusiasm on Holmes' part. Before I could consider the implications of his suggestion, Baskerville had seized Watson by the hand and wrung it heartily.

"Well, now, that is very kind of you, Dr. Watson," said he. "If you will come down to Baskerville Hall and see me through, I'll never forget it."

The promise of adventure—while often a daily occurrence for me—had always a fascination for Watson.

"I will come, with pleasure," said Watson. "I do not know how I could employ my time better."

"And you will report very carefully to me," said Holmes. "When a crisis comes, as it will do, I will direct how you shall act. I suppose that by Saturday all might be ready?"

"Would that suit Dr. Watson?" asked Sir Henry.

"Perfectly."

"Then on Saturday, unless you hear to the contrary, we shall meet at the ten-thirty train from Paddington."

We had risen to depart when Baskerville gave a cry of triumph and, diving into one of the corners of the room, he drew a brown boot from under a cabinet. "My missing boot!" he cried.

"May all our difficulties be solved as easily!" said Sherlock Holmes.

This discovery took me and the others in the room by complete surprise. Since there was virtually no distinguishing odor attached to the new boot, I had not detected its presence upon our return from lunch.

"But it is certainly a very, singular thing," Dr. Mortimer remarked. "I searched this room carefully before lunch."

"And so did I," said Baskerville. "Every inch of it."

"There was certainly no boot in it then."

"In that case the waiter must have placed it there while we were lunching."

The German waiter was sent for, but he professed to know nothing of the matter, nor could any inquiry clear it up.

This, I noted, was another item which had been added to that apparently purposeless series of small mysteries which had succeeded each other so rapidly. Setting aside the whole grim story of Sir Charles's death, we had a line of inexplicable incidents all within the limits of two days. This included the receipt of the printed letter, the spy with the false beard in the hansom, the loss of the new brown boot, the loss of the old black boot, and now the return of the new brown boot.

We sat in silence in the cab as we drove back to Baker Street, and I knew from his drawn brows and keen face that Holmes' mind, like my own, was busy in endeavoring to frame some scheme into which all these strange and apparently disconnected episodes could be fitted.

All afternoon and late into the evening he sat lost in tobacco and thought, while I did my mental work from my worn spot on the hearth-rug.

Just before dinner two telegrams were handed in. Holmes read the first aloud: "Have just heard that Barrymore is at the Hall. Signed, Baskerville."

He then read the second: "Visited twenty-three hotels as

directed, but, sorry to report, unable to trace cut sheet of Times. Signed, Cartwright."

"There go two of our threads," said Holmes as he tossed the telegrams on the table. "There is nothing more stimulating than a case where everything goes against you. We must cast round for another scent."

I looked up at this, thinking Holmes was finally going to send for Toby, but that was not the direction he was headed.

"We have still the cabman who drove the spy," Holmes continued. "I had wired to get his name and address from the Official Registry. I should not be surprised if this were an answer to that particular question."

The ring at the bell proved to be something even more satisfactory than an answer, however, for the door opened and a rough-looking fellow entered. He was evidently the cabman himself.

"I got a message from the head office that a gent at this address had been inquiring for No. 2704," said he as he pulled off his cap and held it against his chest. "I've driven my cab this seven years and never a word of complaint. I came here straight away to ask you to your face what you had against me."

"I have nothing in the world against you, my good man," said Holmes. "On the contrary, I have half a sovereign for you if you will give me a clear answer to my questions."

"Well, I've had a good day and no mistake," said the cabman with a grin. "What was it you wanted to ask, sir?"

"First of all your name and address, in case I want you again."

"John Clayton, 3 Turpey Street, the Borough. My cab is out of Shipley's Yard, near Waterloo Station."

Sherlock Holmes made a note of it.

"Now, Clayton, tell me all about the fare who came and watched this house at ten o'clock this morning and afterwards followed the two gentlemen down Regent Street."

The man looked surprised and a little embarrassed. "Why

there's no good my telling you things, for you seem to know as much as I do already," said he. "The truth is that the gentleman told me that he was a detective and that I was to say nothing about him to anyone."

"You say that your fare told you that he was a detective?"

"Yes, he did."

"Did he say anything more?"

"He mentioned his name."

Holmes cast a swift glance of triumph at me. "Oh, he mentioned his name, did he? That was imprudent. What was the name that he mentioned?"

"His name," said the cabman, "was Mr. Sherlock Holmes."

Never have I seen my master more completely taken aback than by the cabman's reply. For an instant he sat in silent amazement. Then he burst into a hearty laugh.

"A hit—a very palpable hit!" said he. "I feel a foil as quick and supple as my own So his name was Sherlock Holmes, was it?"

"Yes, sir, that was the gentleman's name."

"Excellent! Tell me where you picked him up and all that occurred."

"He hailed me at half-past nine in Trafalgar Square. He said that he was a detective, and he offered me two guineas if I would do exactly what he wanted all day and ask no questions. I was glad enough to agree. First we drove down to the Northumberland Hotel and waited there until two gentlemen came out and took a cab from the rank. We followed their cab until it pulled up somewhere near here."

"This very door," said Holmes.

"Well, I couldn't be sure of that, but I dare say my fare knew all about it. We pulled up halfway down the street and waited an hour and a half. Then the two gentlemen passed us, walking, and we followed down Baker Street and along—"

"I know," said Holmes.

"Until we got three-quarters down Regent Street. Then my

gentleman threw up the trap, and he cried that I should drive right away to Waterloo Station as hard as I could go. I whipped up the mare and we were there in under ten minutes. Then he paid up his two guineas, like a good one, and away he went into the station. Only just as he was leaving he turned round and he said: 'It might interest you to know that you have been driving Mr. Sherlock Holmes.' That's how I come to know the name."

"I see. And you saw no more of him?"

"Not after he went into the station."

"And how would you describe this Mr. Sherlock Holmes?"

The cabman scratched his head. "Well, he wasn't altogether such an easy gentleman to describe. I'd put him at forty years of age, and he was of a middle height, two or three inches shorter than you, sir. He was dressed like a toff, and he had a black beard, cut square at the end, and a pale face. I don't know as I could say more than that."

"Color of his eyes?"

"No, I can't say that."

"Nothing more that you can remember?"

"No, sir; nothing."

"Well, then, here is your half-sovereign. There's another one waiting for you if you can bring any more information. Goodnight!"

"Good-night, sir, and thank you!"

John Clayton departed chuckling, and Holmes turned to us with a shrug of his shoulders and a rueful smile.

"Snap goes our third thread, and we end where we began," said he. "The cunning rascal!"

Indeed. This fellow—whoever he might be—knew our number, knew that Sir Henry Baskerville had consulted us, spotted who Holmes was in Regent Street, conjectured that we had got the number of the cab and would lay our hands on the driver, and so sent back this audacious message. An impressive debut, whoever he might be.

"I tell you," continued Holmes, "this time we have got a foe who is worthy of our steel. I've been checkmated in London. I can only wish you and Septimus better luck in Devonshire. But I'm not easy in my mind about it."

"About what?"

"About sending you two. It's an ugly, dangerous business, and the more I see of it, the less I like it. I give you my word that I shall be very glad to have the two of you back safe and sound in Baker Street once more."

CHAPTER 6

*H*olmes drove with us to the station upon the appointed day and during the ride delivered his last parting injunctions and advice.

Watson listened closely while I looked out the carriage window, excited about the impending trip but secretly wishing Holmes would be coming with us. Dr. Watson is a fine man, but for my money, Holmes is the human you want by your side in a tight situation.

"I will not bias your mind by suggesting theories or suspicions," Holmes was saying when my attention returned to the conversation. "Simply report facts in the fullest possible manner. Leave it to me to do the theorizing."

I wasn't sure what sort of facts he was referring to and I sensed from Watson's expression that he was having the same reaction. However, Holmes had more to say on the topic.

"Especially the relations between young Baskerville and his neighbors or any fresh particulars concerning the death of Sir Charles. One thing only appears to be certain, and that is that Mr. James Desmond, who is the next heir, is an elderly gentleman of a very amiable disposition, so that this persecution does not arise from him. I really think that we may eliminate him entirely from our calculations."

"Would it not be well in the first place to get rid of this Barrymore couple?" asked Watson.

"You could not make a greater mistake. If they are innocent it would be a cruel injustice, and if they are guilty we should be giving up all chance of bringing it home to them. No, no, we will preserve them upon our list of suspects," continued Holmes. "Then there are two moorland farmers. There is our friend Dr. Mortimer, whom I believe to be entirely honest, and there is his wife, of whom we know nothing. There is this naturalist, Stapleton, and there is his sister. There is Mr. Frankland, of Lafter Hall, who is also an unknown factor, and there are one or two other neighbors. These are the folk who must be your very special study."

"I will do my best."

* * *

OUR FRIENDS SIR HENRY AND DR. MORTIMER HAD ALREADY secured a first-class carriage and were waiting for us upon the platform. I was pleased to see that the spaniel was to be a member of our party. We nodded greetings, but—in deference to the professional nature of the encounter—stayed by our respective masters' side.

"No, we have no news of any kind," said Dr. Mortimer in answer to Holmes' questions. "I can swear to one thing, and that is that we have not been shadowed during the last two days. We have never gone out without keeping a sharp watch, and no one could have escaped our notice."

"You have always kept together, I presume?"

"Except yesterday afternoon. I usually give up one day to pure amusement when I come to town, so I spent it at the Museum of the College of Surgeons."

"And I went to look at the folk in the park," said Baskerville.

"But we had no trouble of any kind."

"It was imprudent, all the same," said Holmes, shaking his head and looking very grave. "I beg, Sir Henry, that you will not go about alone. Some great misfortune will befall you if you do. Did you get your other boot?"

"No, sir, it is gone forever."

"Indeed. That is very interesting. Well, good-bye," he added as the train began to glide down the platform. "Bear in mind, Sir Henry, one of the phrases in that queer old legend which Dr. Mortimer has read to us: 'avoid the moor in those hours of darkness when the powers of evil are exalted.'"

I looked back at the platform when we had left it far behind and saw the tall, austere figure of Holmes standing motionless and gazing after us. My eyesight allowed me to look at him longer than others might and it was a long while before he turned from the train and headed back into the station. I have no idea what he was thinking, but the expression I saw until he turned was one of not just consternation, but outright apprehension.

* * *

THE JOURNEY WAS A SWIFT AND PLEASANT ONE. I SPENT ITS entirety gazing out the window, observing the changing landscape as we sailed along. For his part, the spaniel spent the entirety of the trip at Dr. Mortimer's feet, showing virtually no interest in looking out the windows of the speeding train.

Sir Henry Baskerville seemed to share my love of the passing scenery and also stared eagerly out of the window. After much time had passed, he cried aloud with delight as he recognized the familiar features of the Devon scenery.

"I've been over a good part of the world since I left it, Dr. Watson," said he; "but I have never seen a place to compare with it."

"I never saw a Devonshire man who did not swear by his county," remarked Watson.

"I was a boy in my teens at the time of my father's death and had never seen the Hall, for he lived in a little cottage on the South Coast. Thence I went straight to a friend in America. I tell you it is all as new to me as it is to Dr. Watson, and I'm as keen as possible to see the moor."

"Are you? Then your wish is easily granted, for there is your first sight of the moor," said Dr. Mortimer, pointing out of the carriage window.

Over the green squares of the fields and the low curve of a wood there rose in the distance a gray, melancholy hill, with a strange jagged summit, dim and vague in the distance, like some fantastic landscape in a dream. Baskerville sat for a long time his eyes fixed upon it, and I turned from my own study to recognize upon his eager face how much it meant to him, this first sight of that strange spot where the men of his blood had held sway so long.

The train pulled into a small wayside station and we all descended. Outside, beyond the low, white fence, a wagonette with a pair of draft horses was waiting. Our coming was evidently a great event, for the station-master and porters clustered round us to carry out the luggage.

The coachman, a hard-faced, gnarled little fellow, saluted Sir Henry Baskerville, and in a few minutes we were flying swiftly down the broad, white road. Rolling pasture lands curved upward on either side of us, and old gabled houses peeped out from amid the thick green foliage, but behind the peaceful and sunlit countryside there rose ever, dark against the evening sky, the long, gloomy curve of the moor, broken only by the jagged and sinister hills.

The wagonette swung round into a side road, and we curved upward through deep lanes worn by centuries of wheels. Still steadily rising, we passed over a narrow granite bridge and skirted a noisy stream which gushed swiftly down.

At every turn Sir Henry gave an exclamation of delight, looking eagerly about him and asking countless questions. To his eyes all seemed beautiful, but to me a tinge of melancholy lay upon the countryside. Dying leaves carpeted the lanes and fluttered down upon us as we passed. The rattle of our wheels died away as we drove through drifts of rotting vegetation—sad gifts, it seemed to me, for Nature to throw before the carriage of the returning heir of the Baskervilles.

"Halloa!" cried Dr. Mortimer, "what is this?"

On the road ahead, hard and clear like an equestrian statue upon its pedestal, was a mounted soldier, dark and stern, his rifle poised ready over his forearm. He was watching the road along which we travelled.

"What is this, Perkins?" asked Dr. Mortimer.

Our driver half turned in his seat. "There's a convict escaped from Princetown, sir. He's been out three days now, and the warders watch every road and every station, but they've had no sight of him yet. The farmers about here don't like it, sir, and that's a fact."

"Well, I understand that they get five pounds if they can give information."

"Yes, sir, but the chance of five pounds is but a poor thing compared to the chance of having your throat cut. You see, it isn't like any ordinary convict. This is a man that would stick at nothing."

"Who is he, then?"

"It is Selden, the Notting Hill murderer."

I remembered the case well, for it was one in which Holmes had taken an interest on account of the peculiar ferocity of the crime and the wanton brutality which had marked all the actions of the assassin. The commutation of his death sentence had been due to some doubts as to his complete sanity, so atrocious was his conduct.

Our wagonette had topped a rise and in front of us rose the huge expanse of the moor. A cold wind swept down from it and set us shivering. Somewhere there, on that desolate plain, was lurking this fiendish man, hiding in a burrow like a wild beast. Even Baskerville fell silent and pulled his overcoat more closely around him.

I sniffed impotently at the air, knowing full well that with all the new aromas swirling around me—and having no sense of the escaped convict's scent—I was unlikely to produce any useful research results.

We continued on our way. The road in front of us grew bleaker and wilder. Now and then, we passed a moorland cottage, walled and roofed with stone. Suddenly, two high, narrow towers rose over the trees. The driver pointed with his whip.

"Baskerville Hall," said he.

Sir Henry turned and was staring with flushed cheeks and shining eyes. A few minutes later we had reached the lodge-gates.

Through the gateway we passed into the avenue, where the wheels were again hushed amid the leaves. Baskerville shuddered as he looked up the long, dark drive to where the house glimmered like a ghost at the farther end.

"Was it here?" he asked in a low voice.

"No, no, the yew alley is on the other side," Dr. Mortimer explained.

The young heir glanced round with a gloomy face.

"It's no wonder my uncle felt as if trouble were coming on him in such a place as this," said he. "It's enough to scare any man. I'll have a row of electric lamps up here inside of six months, and you won't know it again."

The avenue opened and the house lay before us. In the fading light I could see that the center was a heavy block of building from which a porch projected. The whole front was draped in ivy.

A dull light shone through heavy stone windows, and from the high chimneys which rose from the steep, high-angled roof there sprang a single black column of smoke.

"Welcome, Sir Henry! Welcome to Baskerville Hall!"

A tall man had stepped from the shadow of the porch to open the door of the wagonette. The figure of a woman was silhouetted against the light of the hall. She came out and helped the man to hand down our bags.

"You don't mind my driving straight home, Sir Henry?" said Dr. Mortimer. "My wife is expecting me."

"Surely you will stay and have some dinner?"

"No, I must go. I shall probably find some work awaiting me. I would stay to show you over the house, but Barrymore will be a better guide than I. Good-bye, and never hesitate night or day to send for me if I can be of service."

I bade a silent good-night to the spaniel, who nodded in response, and moments later the wheels died away down the drive while Sir Henry, Watson and I turned into the hall, and the door clanged heavily behind us.

* * *

It was a fine room in which we found ourselves, large, lofty, and heavily raftered with age-blackened oak. In the great old-fashioned fireplace, behind the high iron dogs which I noted were meant to be some breed of hound, a log-fire crackled and snapped.

Sir Henry and Watson held out their hands to it as I stood near the blazing fire, for we were all numb from our long drive. Then we gazed round us at the high, thin windows of old stained glass, the oak paneling, the stags' heads, the coats of arms upon the walls, all dim and somber in the subdued light of the central lamp.

"It's just as I imagined it," said Sir Henry. "Is it not the very picture of an old family home?"

I saw his dark face lit up with a boyish enthusiasm as he gazed about him. Barrymore had returned from taking the luggage to the rooms. He stood in front of us now with the subdued manner of a well-trained servant. He was a remarkable-looking man, tall, handsome, with a square black beard and pale, distinguished features. The beard, I noted immediately, was genuine.

"Would you wish dinner to be served at once, sir?"

"Is it ready?"

"In a very few minutes, sir. You will find hot water in your rooms. My wife and I will be happy, Sir Henry, to stay with you until you have made your fresh arrangements, but you will understand that under the new conditions this house will require a considerable staff."

"What new conditions?"

"I only meant, sir, that Sir Charles led a very retired life, and we were able to look after his wants. You would, naturally, wish to have more company, and so you will need changes in your household."

"Do you mean that your wife and you wish to leave?"

"Only when it is quite convenient to you, sir."

"But your family have been with us for several generations, have they not? I should be sorry to begin my life here by breaking an old family connection."

I seemed to discern some signs of emotion upon the butler's white face.

"I feel that also, sir, and so does my wife. But to tell the truth, sir, we were both very much attached to Sir Charles and his death gave us a shock and made these surroundings very painful to us. I fear that we shall never again be easy in our minds at Baskerville Hall."

"But what do you intend to do?"

"I have no doubt, sir, that we shall succeed in establishing ourselves in some business. Sir Charles's generosity has given us the means to do so. And now, sir, perhaps I had best show you to your rooms."

A square balustraded gallery ran round the top of the old hall, approached by a double stair. From this central point, two long corridors extended the whole length of the building, from which all the bedrooms opened.

The bedroom I was to share with Watson was in the same wing as Baskerville's and almost next door to it. These rooms appeared to be much more modern than the central part of the house, and the bright paper and numerous candles did something to remove the somber impression which our arrival had left upon my mind.

But the dining-room which opened out of the hall was a place of shadow and gloom. A dim line of ancestors, in every variety of dress, from the Elizabethan knight to the flamboyant buck of the Regency, stared down upon us and daunted us by their silent company.

"My word, it isn't a very cheerful place," said Sir Henry. "I don't wonder that my uncle got a little jumpy if he lived all alone in such a house as this. However, if it suits you, we will retire early tonight, and perhaps things may seem more cheerful in the morning."

Watson agreed and moments later he was drawing aside the curtains in our bedroom, affording us both a fine view of the grassy space which lay in front of the hall door. Beyond, two groves of trees moaned and swung in a rising wind. A half-moon broke through the racing clouds. In its cold light, I saw beyond the trees a broken fringe of rocks, and the long, low curve of the melancholy moor.

I found myself weary and yet wakeful, tossing restlessly from side to side at the foot of Watson's bed, seeking the sleep which would not come. Far away a chiming clock struck out the quarters of the hours, but otherwise a deathly silence lay upon the old house.

And then suddenly, in the very dead of the night, there came a sound to my ears, clear, resonant, and unmistakable. It was the sob of a woman, the muffled, strangling gasp of one who is torn by an uncontrollable sorrow.

I sat up suddenly and listened intently. I glanced at the bed, to see the noise had also awakened Watson, who peered into the gloomy room, his hair a shambles atop his head.

The noise could not have been far away and was certainly in the house. Watson soon returned to sleep, but for half an hour I waited with every nerve on the alert.

However, there came no other sound save the chiming of the clock.

CHAPTER 7

*A*s Sir Henry and Watson sat at breakfast, I enjoyed a welcome bowl of kibble nearby, provide by a sad-eyed young maid who seemed exceedingly shy. However, I sensed that she had a fondness for dogs and I was happy to benefit from her largesse.

The sunlight flooded in through the high mullioned windows, throwing watery patches of light from the coats of arms which covered them.

"It's hard to realize that this is indeed the same house which had struck such gloom into our souls last evening," Watson commented, echoing my sentiments precisely.

"I guess it is ourselves and not the house that we have to blame!" said the baronet. "We were tired with our journey and chilled by our drive, so we took a gray view of the place. Now we are fresh and well, so it is all cheerful once more."

"And yet it was not entirely a question of imagination," Watson answered. "Did you, for example, happen to hear someone, a woman I think, sobbing in the night?"

"That is curious, for I did when I was half asleep, fancy that I heard something of the sort. I waited quite a time, but there was no more of it, so I concluded that it was all a dream."

"I heard it distinctly," said Watson, "and I am sure that it was really the sob of a woman." He glanced down at me, for he knew I had detected the sound before he and it was my response to it that had made the distant wail all the more real to him.

"We must ask about this right away," said Sir Henry as he rang the bell and asked Barrymore whether he could account for our experience. It seemed to me that, even in the bright sunlight which streamed through the windows, the pallid features of the butler turned a shade paler still as he listened to his master's question.

"There are only two women in the house, Sir Henry," he answered. "One is the scullery-maid, who sleeps in the other wing. The other is my wife, and I can answer for it that the sound could not have come from her."

And yet he lied as he said it, for it chanced that after breakfast Watson and I met Mrs. Barrymore in the long corridor with the sun full upon her face. She was a large, impassive, heavy-featured woman with a stern set expression of mouth. But her telltale eyes were discolored and glanced at us from between swollen lids. While I have not yet mastered the art of detecting the myriad of human emotions, it would have been clear even to the spaniel that this woman had spent the better part of the night crying.

It was she, then, who wept in the night, and if she did so her husband must know it. Yet he had taken the obvious risk of discovery in declaring that it was not so. Why had he done this? And why did she weep so bitterly?

I looked to Watson and could tell that, although he may not be asking the same questions himself, he at least recognized the subterfuge and had made note of it.

* * *

Sir Henry had numerous papers to examine after breakfast, and so I was delighted to see that Watson had decided the time was propitious for an excursion. It was a pleasant walk of four miles along the edge of the moor, leading us at last to a small gray village, in which two larger buildings—which proved to be the inn and the house of Dr. Mortimer—stood high above the rest.

When questioned by Watson, the postmaster, who was also the village grocer, had a clear recollection of the telegram which Holmes had sent to Barrymore. A detailed conversation ensued, which included the participation of his boy, James, who had made the actual delivery of the telegram.

However, upon further questioning, it was determined the wire had gone to Mrs. Barrymore, who promised to give it to her husband when he came down from the loft.

Still more conversation ensued, none of which was of interest to me, as I was entirely certain it had not been Barrymore whom we had spotted in London.

So while Watson and the postmaster went back and forth on the topic, I wandered the small shop, which held a mix of familiar and unfamiliar smells. I was just examining some odd spices which had fallen on the floor—perhaps coriander, although I could have sworn it was cilantro—when Watson tracked me down, his interrogation apparently completed.

Watson mumbled to himself as we left the small village and I sensed he was replaying the events of the last few days through his mind. Holmes himself had said that no more complex case had come to him in all the long series of his sensational investigations, and so I think Watson can be forgiven for any trouble he was experiencing trying to hold all the pieces in his mind.

I prayed, as we walked back along the gray, lonely road, that Holmes might soon be freed from his preoccupations and able to come down to take this heavy burden of responsibility from Watson's shoulders. Clearly the good doctor was burdened by the duties Holmes had bestowed upon him.

Suddenly these thoughts were interrupted by the sound of running feet behind us and by a voice which called Watson by name. It was an unfamiliar voice, and I turned to see it was a stranger who was pursuing us. He was a small, slim, clean-shaven, prim-faced man, between thirty and forty years of age, dressed in a gray suit and wearing a straw hat. A tin box hung over his shoulder and he carried a butterfly-net in one of his hands.

"You will, I am sure, excuse my presumption, Dr. Watson," said he as he came panting up to where we stood. "Here on the moor we are simple folk and do not wait for formal introductions. You may possibly have heard my name from our mutual friend, Dr. Mortimer. I am Stapleton, of Merripit House."

"Your net and box would have told me as much," said Watson, "for I knew that Mr. Stapleton was a naturalist. But how did you know me?"

"I had been calling on Mortimer, and he pointed you out to me from the window of his surgery as you passed. As our road lay the same way I thought that I would overtake you and introduce myself. And who is this fine specimen?" he asked, looking down in my direction.

"Ah, yes," said Watson, perhaps remembering that I had been faithfully trotting at his side. "This is Septimus. He belongs to Holmes," he added, with an unnecessary pat atop my head. I tolerated the patronizing nature of the action, but just barely.

"A courser, was he?"

"Well, yes, I believe he was," Watson stammered. "I believe he was a gift from someone in the Swaffham Coursing Society, although I forget the details."

The word *gift* was, to my mind, a misnomer.

While in the midst of a case in that vicinity, Holmes had spotted me—and I him—and we had joined forces, as he'd required an assistant with speed, brains and excellent eye-sight. Despite my young age, he felt I fit the bill exceedingly well. As he said at the time, quoting the poet Augustus, a greyhound is "swifter than thought."

Someday, if he gets around to it, Holmes may dictate the details of that adventure, and Watson can add it to his literary trove.

"And you both came down, with Sir Henry?" continued Stapleton.

"Yes, we arrived last evening."

"I trust that Sir Henry is none the worse for his journey?"

"He is very well, thank you."

"We were all rather afraid that after the sad death of Sir Charles, the new baronet might refuse to live here. It is asking much of a wealthy man to come down and bury himself in a place of this kind, but I need not tell you that it means a very great deal to the countryside. Sir Henry has, I suppose, no superstitious fears in the matter?"

"I do not think that it is likely."

"Of course you know the legend of the fiendish hound which haunts the family?"

"I have heard it," said Watson.

My ears perked up at the mention of the hound. I was curious to hear what others thought of the tale.

"It is extraordinary how credulous the peasants are about here," continued Stapleton. "Any number of them are ready to swear that they have seen such a creature upon the moor." He spoke with a smile, but I seemed to read in his eyes that he took the matter more seriously. "The story took a great hold upon the imagination of Sir Charles, and I have no doubt that it led to his tragic end."

"But how?"

"His nerves were so worked up that the appearance of any dog might have had a fatal effect upon his diseased heart. I fancy that he really did see something of the kind upon that last night in the yew alley. I feared that some disaster might occur, for I was very fond of the old man, and I knew that his heart was weak."

"How did you know that?"

"My friend Mortimer told me."

"You think, then, that some dog pursued Sir Charles, and that he died of fright in consequence?"

"Have you any better explanation?"

"I have not come to any conclusion."

"Has Mr. Sherlock Holmes?"

The words took away Watson's breath for an instant, but a glance at Stapleton's placid face and steadfast eyes showed that no surprise was intended.

"It is useless for us to pretend that we do not know you, Dr. Watson," said he. "The records of your detective have reached us here, and you could not celebrate him without being known yourself. If you are here, then it follows that Mr. Sherlock Holmes is interested in the matter, and I am naturally curious to know what view he may take."

"I am afraid that I cannot answer that question."

"May I ask if he is going to honor us with a visit himself?"

"He cannot leave town at present. He has other cases which engage his attention."

"What a pity! He might throw some light on that which is so dark to us. But as to your own researches, if there is any possible way in which I can be of service to you, I trust that you will command me."

"I assure you that I am simply here upon a visit to my friend, Sir Henry, and that I need no help of any kind."

"Excellent!" said Stapleton. "You are perfectly right to be wary and discreet. I promise you that I will not mention the matter again."

We had come to a point where a narrow grassy path struck off from the road and wound away across the moor.

"A moderate walk along this moor-path brings us to Merripit

House," said Stapleton. "Perhaps you will spare an hour that I may have the pleasure of introducing you to my sister."

My first thought was that we should be by Sir Henry's side. But then I remembered the pile of papers and bills with which his study table was littered. It was certain that Watson and I would be of absolutely no help with those, unless his goal was to tear up the papers and scatter them about the room in random fashion. I could certainly assist in an endeavor of that sort. But that was an unlikely request. And Holmes had expressly said that we should study the neighbors upon the moor.

I'm not sure if Watson's train of thought travelled along similar lines, but he accepted Stapleton's invitation, and we turned together down the path.

"It is a wonderful place, the moor," said Stapleton. "You never tire of the moor. You cannot imagine the wonderful secrets which it contains. It is so vast, and so barren, and so mysterious."

"You know it well, then?"

"I have only been here two years. The residents would call me a newcomer. We came shortly after Sir Charles settled. But my tastes led me to explore every part of the country round, and I should think that there are few men who know it better than I do."

"Is it hard to know?"

"Very hard. You see, for example, this great plain to the north here with the queer hills breaking out of it. Do you observe anything remarkable about that?"

"It would be a rare place for a gallop," said Watson.

I had to agree, as it looked to be an ideal spot to break into a sprint, as it was so open and green. Such opportunities are rare indeed in London proper, although once or twice Holmes has let me off the leash in Greenwich Park, on his occasional visits to the Royal Observatory.

"You would naturally think so and the thought has cost several their lives before now. You notice those bright green spots scattered thickly over it?"

"Yes, they seem more fertile than the rest."

Stapleton laughed. "That is the great Grimpen Mire," said he. "A false step yonder means death to man or beast. Only yesterday I saw one of the moor ponies wander into it. He never came out. Even in dry seasons it is a danger to cross it, but after these autumn rains it is an awful place. And yet I can find my way to the very heart of it and return alive. But, it's a bad place, the great Grimpen Mire."

"And you say you can penetrate it?"

"Yes, there are one or two paths which a very active man can take. It is only by remembering certain complex landmarks that I am able to do it."

"Halloa!" I cried. "What is that?"

A long, low moan, indescribably sad, swept over the moor. It filled the whole air, and yet it was impossible to say from where it came. From a dull murmur it swelled into a deep roar, and then sank back into a melancholy, throbbing murmur once again. Stapleton looked at us with a curious expression in his face.

"Queer place, the moor!" said he.

"But what was that?"

"The peasants say it is the Hound of the Baskervilles calling for its prey. I've heard it once or twice before, but never quite so loud."

I looked round, with a chill in my heart, at the huge expansive plain, mottled with patches of rushes. Nothing stirred save a pair of ravens, which croaked loudly from behind us. I gave the air a quick sniff, which offered no immediate inklings as to the source of the sound, which was wholly unfamiliar to me.

"You are an educated man. You don't believe such nonsense as that?" said Watson. "What do you think is the cause of so strange a sound?"

"Bogs make queer noises sometimes. It's the mud settling, or the water rising, or something."

"No, no, that was a living voice. It's the weirdest, strangest thing that ever I heard in my life."

I had to agree with Watson on that point; I had never heard anything like it.

"Yes, it's rather an uncanny place altogether," agreed Stapleton.

A small fly or moth fluttered across our path, and in an instant Stapleton was rushing with extraordinary energy and speed in pursuit of it.

To my dismay the creature flew straight for the great mire, and yet the man never paused for an instant, bounding from tuft to tuft behind it, his net waving in the air.

I was watching his pursuit with a mixture of admiration for his extraordinary activity and fear lest he should lose his footing in the treacherous mire, where I knew Watson would be unable to pull him free.

I heard the sound of steps behind us, and turning round, found a woman near us upon the path. She had come from the direction in which the plume of smoke indicated the position of Merripit House, but the dip of the moor had hidden her until she was quite close.

I felt no doubt this was the Miss Stapleton of whom we had been told, since I understood ladies of any sort must be few upon the moor.

She had a proud, finely cut face, so regular that it might have seemed impassive were it not for the sensitive mouth and the dark, eager eyes. Those eyes were on her brother as I turned, and then she quickened her pace towards us. Watson had raised his hat and was about to make some explanatory remark when her own words turned all my thoughts into a new channel.

"Go back!" she said to Watson, although I felt her comment was directed equally at the both of us. "Go straight back to London, instantly."

Watson stared at her in stupid surprise. Her eyes blazed at him, and she tapped the ground impatiently with her foot.

"Why should we go back?" asked Watson.

"I cannot explain." She spoke in a low, eager voice. "But for God's sake, do what I ask you. Go back and never set foot upon the moor again."

"But we have only just come."

"Can you not tell when a warning is for your own good?" she cried. "Go back to London! Start tonight! Get away from this place at all costs! Hush, my brother is coming! Not a word of what I have said."

Stapleton had abandoned the chase and came back to us, breathing hard and flushed with his exertions.

"Halloa, Beryl!" said he, and it seemed to me that the tone of his greeting was not altogether a cordial one.

"Well, Jack, you are very hot."

"Yes, I was chasing a Cyclopides. He is very rare and seldom found in the late autumn. What a pity that I should have missed him!" He spoke unconcernedly, but his small eyes glanced incessantly from the girl to Watson and me.

"You have introduced yourselves, I can see," said Stapleton.

"Yes. I was telling Sir Henry that it was rather late for him to see the true beauties of the moor," she said.

"Why, who do you think this is?"

She looked surprised at the question. "I imagine that it must be Sir Henry Baskerville."

"No, no," said Watson. "Only a humble commoner, but his friend. My name is Dr. Watson. And this is Septimus," he added, gesturing in my direction.

A flush of vexation passed over her expressive face. "We have been talking at cross purposes," said she.

"Why, you had not very much time for talk," her brother remarked.

"I talked as if Dr. Watson were a resident instead of being

merely a visitor," said she. "But you will come on, will you not, and see Merripit House?"

* * *

A SHORT WALK BROUGHT US TO IT, A BLEAK HOUSE, ONCE A FARM IN the old prosperous days, but now turned into a modern dwelling. An orchard surrounded it, but the trees, as is usual upon the moor, were stunted and the effect of the whole place was melancholy.

We were admitted into the house by a strange, wizened, rusty-coated old manservant, who seemed in keeping with the house. Inside, however, there were large rooms furnished with elegance. As I studied the room, I could not but marvel at what could have brought this highly-educated man and this fiercely intelligent woman to live in such a place.

"Queer spot to choose, is it not?" said Stapleton as if in answer to my thought. "And yet we manage to make ourselves fairly happy, do we not, Beryl?"

"Quite happy," said she, but there was no ring of conviction in her words.

"I find an unlimited field of work here," said Stapleton, "and my sister is as devoted to Nature as I am. We have books, we have our studies, and we have interesting neighbors. Dr. Mortimer is a most learned man in his own line. Poor Sir Charles was also an admirable companion. We knew him well and miss him more than I can tell. Do you think that I should intrude if I were to call this afternoon and make the acquaintance of Sir Henry?"

"I am sure that he would be delighted."

"Then perhaps you would mention that I propose to do so? We may in our humble way do something to make things more easy for him until he becomes accustomed to his new surroundings. Will you come upstairs, Dr. Watson, and inspect my collection of

Lepidoptera? By the time that you have looked through them, lunch will be almost ready."

Watson hesitated, unsure how to respond. I gave the slightest pull on my leash, as I was eager to get back to our charge. The melancholy of the moor, the death of the unfortunate pony, the weird sound which had been associated with the grim legend of the Baskervilles, all these things filled my mind.

Then on top of these more or less vague impressions, there had come the definite and distinct warning of Miss Stapleton, delivered with such intense earnestness that I could not doubt that some grave and deep reason lay behind it.

My slight, nearly imperceptible tug on the leash was enough to sway Watson and, after quick good-byes, we set off at once upon our return journey, taking the grass-grown path by which we had come.

It seems, however, that there must have been some short cut for those who knew it, for before we had reached the road, I was astounded to see Miss Stapleton sitting upon a rock by the side of the track. Her face was flushed with her exertions and she held her hand to her side.

"I have run all the way in order to cut you off," said she. "I had not even time to put on my hat. I must not stop, or my brother may miss me. I wanted to say to you how sorry I am about the stupid mistake I made in thinking that you were Sir Henry. Please forget the words I said, which have no application whatever to you."

"But I can't forget them, Miss Stapleton," said Watson. "I am Sir Henry's friend, and his welfare is a very close concern of mine. Tell me why you were so eager that Sir Henry should return to London."

"A woman's whim, Dr. Watson. When you know me better you will understand that I cannot always give reasons for what I say or do."

"No, no. I remember the emotion in your voice. I remember

the look in your eyes. Please, please, be frank with me, Miss Stapleton," said Watson, "for ever since we have been here, I have been conscious of shadows all round me. Life has become like that great Grimpen Mire, with little green patches everywhere into which one may sink and with no guide to point the track. Tell me then what it was that you meant, and I will promise to convey your warning to Sir Henry."

An expression of irresolution passed for an instant over her face, but her eyes had hardened again when she answered him.

"You make too much of it, Dr. Watson," said she. "My brother and I were very much shocked by the death of Sir Charles. We knew him very intimately, for his favorite walk was over the moor to our house. He was deeply impressed with the curse which hung over the family, and when this tragedy came I naturally felt that there must be some grounds for the fears which he had expressed. I was distressed, therefore, when another member of the family came down to live here. I felt that he should be warned of the danger which he will run."

"But what is the danger?"

"You know the story of the hound?"

"I do not believe in such nonsense."

"But I do. If you have any influence with Sir Henry, take him away from this place which has always been fatal to his family."

"I fear that unless you can give me some more definite information than this, it would be impossible to get him to move."

"I cannot say anything definite, for I do not know anything definite."

"I would ask you one more question, Miss Stapleton. Why should you not wish your brother to overhear what you said?"

"My brother is very anxious to have the Hall inhabited, for he thinks it is for the good of the poor folk upon the moor. He would be very angry if he knew that I have said anything which might induce Sir Henry to go away. But I have done my duty now and I will say no more. I must go back, or he will miss me and suspect that I have seen you. Good-bye!"

She turned and had disappeared in a few seconds among the scattered boulders.

With more questions than answers filling my mind, Watson and I pursued our way back towards Baskerville Hall.

CHAPTER 8

$\mathcal{T}$he next few days offered little real progress in the case. There were, of course, many discussions concerning the escaped convict, who came up as a topic at virtually every meal.

"There is strong reason now to believe that he has gotten away," said Sir Henry at one dinner, "which is a considerable relief to the lonely householders of this district. A fortnight has passed since his flight, during which he has not been seen and nothing has been heard of him."

"It is surely inconceivable that he could have held out upon the moor during all that time," said Watson.

"It is unlikely," said Baskerville. "There is nothing to eat unless he were to catch and slaughter one of the moor sheep. We think, therefore, that he has gone, and the outlying farmers sleep the better in consequence."

"I certainly hope so."

"We are four able-bodied men in this household," continued Sir Henry, "so that we could take good care of ourselves, but I confess that I have had uneasy moments when I have thought of the Stapletons."

While I understood Sir Henry's concern for the brother and sister—they live miles from any help, they have but one maid and an old manservant, and the brother is not a very strong man—it was also, I noted, in keeping with his growing interest in Beryl Stapleton.

I think Watson noticed this as well, but he talked around the issue.

"Yes, they would be helpless in the hands of a desperate fellow like this Notting Hill criminal if he could force an entrance."

"I agree," said Sir Henry. "I suggested that Perkins the groom should go over to sleep there, but Stapleton would not hear of it."

In truth, I was not surprised that our friend, the baronet, had begun to display a considerable interest in his fair neighbor. Time hangs heavily in this lonely spot to an active man like him, and she is a very fascinating woman and, I suspect although I cannot claim it, beautiful within the human definition of the word.

One thing I had noticed, in my limited encounters with the siblings, was the marked influence Stapleton held over her. I had seen her continually glance at him as she talked, as if seeking approbation for what she said. He possessed a dark look in his eyes and a firm set of his thin lips, which often goes with a possibly a harsh nature—the owner of the kennel from which Holmes rescued me had a similar sharp expression. Were he here, I believe Holmes would find Stapleton an interesting study.

* * *

As he had promised, Stapleton came over to call upon Baskerville on that first day, and the very next morning he showed us the spot where the legend of the wicked Hugo is supposed to have had its origin. It was an excursion of some miles across the moor, to a place which was so dismal that it might have suggested the story. The hike was longer than most of my jaunts with Holmes and I think the same must have been true of Watson, for we both were winded by the journey and did our best to keep up with Stapleton and our host.

The location in every way corresponded with the scene of the old tragedy. Sir Henry was much interested and he asked Stapleton more than once whether he did really believe in the possibility of the interference of the supernatural in the affairs of men. He spoke lightly, but it was evident that he was very much in earnest.

Stapleton appeared guarded in his replies, but it was easy to see that he said less than he might, and that he would not express his whole opinion out of consideration for the feelings of the baronet. He told us of similar cases, where families had suffered from some evil influence, and he left us with the impression that he shared the popular view upon the matter.

For myself, while the terrain was eerie and the air itself was fetid and musty, it seemed to me—as it always does—that the answers were more likely to be found firmly on the natural realm. Watson, for his part, stayed silent, still puffing from the march.

On our way back we stayed for lunch at Stapleton's home, Merripit House, and it was there that Sir Henry made his first acquaintance of Miss Stapleton.

From the first moment that he saw her, he appeared to be strongly attracted by her, and I am much mistaken if the feeling was not mutual. He referred to her again and again on our walk home, and since then hardly a day has passed that we have not seen something of the brother and sister.

Although I don't claim complete understanding of human mating rituals, I would imagine that such a match would be very welcome to Stapleton. And yet I have more than once caught a look of the strongest displeasure in his face when Sir Henry has been paying some attention to his sister. He is much attached to her, no doubt, and would lead a lonely life without her, but it would seem the height of selfishness if he were to stand in the way of her finding happiness in marriage.

It then occurred to me that—if Sir Henry were to begin a relationship with the Stapleton woman—we would have great difficulty in following Holmes' instructions to never allow Sir Henry to go out alone. In point of fact, I believe our popularity with the baronet would suffer if we attempted to follow my master's orders to the letter.

* * *

DR. MORTIMER, WHO HAD BEEN MISSING FROM OUR COMPANY FOR several days, lunched with us and I was delighted to discover he had brought his spaniel along. The pup greeted me like a long-lost friend and although I responded with enthusiasm, my response was the more tempered of the two. We shared a bowl of kitchen scraps while the humans dined and then we rested while they talked of events in the village. The search for the convict had dwindled to nothing and attention had turned to the change of season.

The Stapletons came in afterwards and the conversation soon turned to the other neighbors Sir Henry had yet to meet.

One such neighbor was Mr. Frankland, of Lafter Hall, who lives some four miles to the south of the Baskerville estate. Watson and I had met him—oh so briefly—on a long walk two days earlier, but Mortimer knew him quite well. Watson let the good doctor describe the curious old man.

"He is an elderly man, red-faced, white-haired, and choleric," explained Dr. Mortimer. "His passion is for the British law, and he has spent a large fortune in litigation. He fights for the mere pleasure of fighting and is equally ready to take up either side of a question, so that it is no wonder that he has found it a costly amusement."

"Yes," agreed Watson. "In the short conversation we exchanged, he mentioned more than one lawsuit with which he was in active litigation."

"He is said to have about seven lawsuits upon his hands at present," added Stapleton, "which will probably swallow up the remainder of his fortune and so draw his sting and leave him harmless for the future."

"Apart from the law, he seems a kindly, good-natured person," added his sister. "He is curiously employed at present, for, being an amateur astronomer, he has an excellent telescope. With it, he lies upon the roof of his own house and sweeps the moor all day in the hope of catching a glimpse of the escaped convict."

"If he would confine his energies to that endeavor, all would be well," continued Mortimer. "But in his own curious way, he helps to keep our lives from being monotonous and gives a little comic relief where it is badly needed."

After that discussion, the good doctor took us all to the yew alley at Sir Henry's request, to show us exactly how everything occurred upon that fatal night. It is a long, dismal walk between two high walls of clipped hedge, with a narrow band of grass upon either side. At the far end is an old tumble-down summer-house. Halfway down is the moor-gate, where the old gentleman left his cigar-ash. It is a white wooden gate with a latch. Beyond it lies the wide moor.

While we stood there, I remembered Holmes' theory of the affair and tried to picture all that had occurred. As the old man stood there, he saw something coming across the moor, something which terrified him so that he lost his wits and ran and ran until he died of sheer horror and exhaustion.

There was the long, gloomy tunnel down which he fled. And from what? A sheep-dog of the moor? Or a spectral hound, black, silent, and monstrous? Was there a human agency in the matter?

I sniffed the air, but of course any clue had long since wafted away; I doubt even Toby himself would have found evidence of any kind this long after the fatal event.

* * *

LATER THAT DAY, SIR HENRY RAISED THE QUESTION OF Barrymore's whereabouts during the baronet's time in the city. Watson explained to Sir Henry how the matter stood, and he at once, in his downright fashion, had Barrymore up and asked him whether he had received the telegram himself. Barrymore said that he had.

"Did the boy deliver it into your own hands?" asked Sir Henry.

Barrymore looked surprised, and considered for a little time.

"No," said he, "I was in the box-room at the time, and my wife brought it up to me."

"Did you answer it yourself?"

"No; I told my wife what to answer and she went down to write it." There was a long moment of silence, and then Barrymore continued. "I do not quite understand the object of your questions, Sir Henry," said he. "I trust that they do not mean that I have done anything to forfeit your confidence?"

Sir Henry assured him that it was not so and, had I the gift of speech, I could have rectified the question in a moment. But still, it was of interest to me to see Barrymore's reaction to the questioning.

Mrs. Barrymore is also of interest to me. She is a heavy, solid person. You could hardly conceive a less emotional subject. Yet I know on the first night here, I heard her sobbing bitterly, and since then I have more than once observed traces of tears upon her face. Some deep sorrow gnaws ever at her heart.

Sometimes I wonder if she has a guilty memory which haunts her, and sometimes I suspect Barrymore of being a domestic tyrant. I have always felt that there was something singular and questionable in this man's character, but my next adventure with the man brought all my suspicions to a head.

* * *

I AM NOT A VERY SOUND SLEEPER, AND SINCE I HAVE BEEN ON GUARD in this house my slumbers have been lighter than ever. Last night, about two in the morning, I was aroused by a stealthy step passing the room I share with Dr. Watson. I rose and pushed against the bedroom door, only to find it securely latched.

With no other recourse before me, and time being of the essence, I returned to the bed and pressed my nose against the back of Dr. Watson's sleeping neck. The sudden cold, wet pressure did the trick and moments later he was on his feet.

"Need to go out, old man?" he grumbled as he threw on his robe.

Moments later, we were at the door to the bedroom, which he opened with an enviable ease. I took one step in front of him and then stopped, turning my head to indicate where I needed him to look. Watson, for all his faults, is far easier to lead than Holmes, as experience has taught me.

A long black shadow was trailing down the corridor. It was thrown by a man who walked softly down the passage with a candle held in his hand. He was in shirt and trousers, with no covering to his feet. I could merely see the outline, but his height told me that it was Barrymore.

Watson must have agreed, as a moment later I heard him whisper that same name aloud.

We waited until he had passed out of sight and then I followed him, with Watson one step behind me. When we came round the balcony, Barrymore had reached the end of the farther corridor, and I could see from the glimmer of light through an open door that he had entered one of the rooms. Now, all these rooms are unfurnished and unoccupied, so that his expedition became more mysterious than ever. The light shone steadily as if he were standing motionless. We crept down the passage as noiselessly as we could and peeped round the corner of the door.

Barrymore was crouching at the window with the candle held against the glass. His profile was half turned towards us, and his face seemed to be rigid with expectation as he stared out into the blackness of the moor. For some minutes he stood watching intently. Then he gave a deep groan and with an impatient gesture he put out the light.

Instantly we made our way back to our room, and very shortly came the stealthy steps passing once more upon their return journey.

Long afterwards, when Watson had fallen back into a light sleep, I heard a key turn somewhere in a lock. And then the sound of a door opening and closing.

I could not tell from where the sound came.

CHAPTER 9

*B*efore breakfast on the morning following our late-night adventure, Watson and I went down the corridor and examined the room in which Barrymore had been on the night before. That is to say, when he opened the bedroom door, I headed in that direction and Watson gamely followed.

The western window through which Barrymore had stared so intently has, I noticed, one with a peculiarity above all other windows in the house—it commanded the clearest outlook on to the moor.

There is an opening between two trees which enables one from that point of view to look right down upon the moor, while from all the other windows it is only a distant glimpse which can be obtained. It follows, therefore, that Barrymore, since only this window would serve the purpose, must have been looking out for something or someone upon the moor.

The night had been very dark, so that I can hardly imagine how he could have hoped to see anyone. It had struck me that it was possible that some love intrigue was afoot. That would have accounted for his stealthy movements and also for the uneasiness of his wife.

The opening and closing of a door which I had heard after I had returned to our room might mean that he had gone out to keep some clandestine appointment.

But whatever the true explanation of Barrymore's movements might be, Watson must have felt that the responsibility of keeping them to himself was more than he could bear. At breakfast with Sir Henry, Watson told him all that we had seen.

The baronet was less surprised than I had expected.

"I knew that Barrymore walked about nights, and I had a mind to speak to him about it," said he. "Two or three times I have heard his steps in the passage, coming and going, just about the hour you name."

"Perhaps then he pays a visit every night to that particular window," suggested Watson.

"Perhaps he does. If so, we should be able to shadow him and see what it is that he is after. I wonder what your friend Holmes would do if he were here?"

"I believe that he would do exactly what you now suggest," said Watson with a glance down in my direction. "He would follow Barrymore and see what he did."

"Then we shall do it together."

"But surely he would hear us."

"The man is rather deaf, and in any case we must take our chance of that. We'll sit up in my room tonight and wait until he passes."

Sir Henry rubbed his hands with pleasure, and it was evident to me that he hailed the adventure as a relief to his somewhat quiet life upon the moor.

* * *

AFTER BREAKFAST, SIR HENRY PUT ON HIS HAT AND PREPARED TO GO out. I picked up my leash and brought it to Watson, who immediately understood the signal and picked up his own hat.

"What, are you coming, Watson?" Sir Henry asked, looking at us in a curious way.

"That depends on whether you are going on the moor," said Watson.

"Yes, I am."

"Well, you know what our instructions are. I am sorry to intrude, but you heard how earnestly Holmes insisted that we should not leave you, and especially that you should not go alone upon the moor."

Sir Henry put his hand upon Watson's shoulder with a pleasant smile.

"My dear fellow," said he, "Holmes, with all his wisdom, did not foresee some things which have happened since I have been on the moor. You understand me? I am sure that you are the last man in the world who would wish to be a spoil-sport. I must go out alone."

Watson appeared to be at a loss what to say or what to do, and before I could take any action, Sir Henry picked up his cane and was gone.

Watson looked blankly at the closed door before him, seemingly frozen into inactivity. I had already lain the leash at his feet and saw no other recourse but to break the spell with the only other reasonable tool at my disposal.

I barked, once, loudly.

Short of biting him on the leg, it felt like the only option before me—and be assured, a nip on the leg would have been my next action. However, the sudden, loud and uncharacteristic bark seemed to turn the trick, as moments later—with leash in hand—we pushed our way through the front door and set off at once in the direction of Merripit House.

* * *

WE HURRIED ALONG THE ROAD—AT WATSON'S TOP SPEED, NOT MY

own—without seeing anything of Sir Henry, until we came to the point where the moor path branches off.

There, fearing that perhaps I had led us in the wrong direction after all, we mounted a hill from which we could command a view —the same hill which is cut into the dark quarry. There I saw him at once. He was on the moor path about a quarter of a mile off, and a lady was by his side who, my sharp eyesight assured me, was Miss Stapleton.

It was clear that there was an understanding between them and that they had met by appointment. They were walking slowly along in deep conversation, and I saw her making quick little movements of her hands as if she were very earnest in what she was saying, while he listened intently, and once or twice shook his head in strong dissent.

We stood among the rocks watching them, very much puzzled as to what we should do next. To follow them and break into their intimate conversation seemed to be an outrage, and yet our clear duty was never for an instant to let him out of our sight.

Our friend, Sir Henry, and the lady halted on the path and were standing deeply absorbed in their conversation, when I was suddenly aware that Watson and I were not the only witnesses of their interview.

A wisp of netting floating in the air caught my eye, and another glance showed me that it was carried on a stick by a man who was moving among the broken ground. It was Stapleton with his butterfly-net. He was very much closer to the pair than we were and he appeared to be moving in their direction.

At this instant, Sir Henry suddenly drew Miss Stapleton to his side. Stapleton was running wildly towards them, his absurd net dangling behind him. He gesticulated and almost danced with excitement in front of the lovers. What the scene meant I could not imagine, but it seemed to me that Stapleton was abusing Sir Henry, who offered explanations, which became more angry as the other refused to accept them. The lady stood by in stony silence.

Finally Stapleton turned upon his heel and beckoned in a peremptory way to his sister, who, after an irresolute glance at Sir Henry, walked off by the side of her brother. The naturalist's angry gestures showed that the lady was included in his displeasure.

The baronet stood for a minute looking after them, and then he walked slowly back the way that he had come, his head hanging, the very picture of dejection.

What all this meant I could not imagine, as my judgement of human emotions ranks far below my other keen senses.

Watson, who seemed to feel no such confusion as to the scene we had witnessed, headed toward the baronet, whose face was flushed with anger and his brows were wrinkled, like one who is at his wit's ends what to do.

"Halloa, Watson! Where have you dropped from?" said he. "You don't mean to say that you and Septimus came after me in spite of it all?"

Watson explained everything to him: how we had found it impossible to remain behind, how we had followed him, and how we had witnessed all that had occurred. For an instant Sir Henry's eyes blazed at the two of us, but Watson's frankness disarmed his anger, and he broke at last into a rather rueful laugh.

"You would have thought the middle of that prairie a fairly safe place for a man to be private," said he. "But, by thunder, the whole countryside seems to have been out to see me do my wooing— and a mighty poor wooing at that! Where had you engaged a seat?"

"We were on that hill."

"Quite in the back row, eh? But her brother was well up to the front. Did you see him come out on us?"

"Yes, we did," said Watson, although he had not actually seen him until the sharp turn of my head indicated the man's presence.

And I doubt he observed the scene with the same clarity my eyesight brought to the occasion.

"Did he ever strike you as being crazy—this brother of hers?" asked Sir Henry.

"I can't say that he ever did."

"I always thought him sane enough until today, but you can take it from me that either he or I ought to be in a straitjacket. What's the matter with me, anyhow? You've lived near me for some weeks, Watson. Tell me straight, now! Is there anything that would prevent me from making a good husband to a woman that I loved?"

"I should say not."

"He can't object to my worldly position, so it must be myself that he is down on. What has he against me? I never hurt man or woman in my life that I know of. And yet he would not so much as let me touch the tips of her fingers."

"Did he say so?"

"That, and a good deal more. Just tell me what it all means, Watson, and I'll owe you more than I can ever hope to pay."

Watson offered one or two explanations, but, indeed, he was as completely puzzled as I was.

However, the conjectures were set at rest by a visit from Stapleton himself that very afternoon. He had come to offer apologies for his rudeness of the morning, and after a long private interview with Sir Henry in his study, the upshot of their conversation was that the breach was quite healed, and that we are to dine at Merripit House next Friday as a sign of it.

"I don't say now that he isn't a crazy man," said Sir Henry after Stapleton had departed. "I can't forget the look in his eyes when he ran at me this morning. But I must allow that no man could make a more handsome apology than he has done."

"Did he give any explanation of his conduct?" asked Watson.

"His sister is everything in his life, he says. They have always been together, and according to his account he has been a very lonely man with only her as a companion, so that the thought of losing her was really terrible to him," Sir Henry said. "He explained he would withdraw all opposition upon his part if I would promise for three months to let the matter rest and to be content with cultivating the lady's friendship during that time without claiming her love. This I promised, and so the matter rests."

* * *

THE TOPIC THEN MOVED TO "OUR NIGHT'S WORK," BUT, IN TRUTH, IT was two nights' work, for on the first night we drew entirely blank.

Watson and I sat up with Sir Henry in his rooms until nearly three o'clock in the morning on that first night, but no sound of any sort did we hear, except the chiming clock upon the stairs. It was a most melancholy vigil and ended by the two men falling asleep in their chairs while I kept watch at their feet.

Fortunately they were not discouraged, and they determined to try again.

The next night Sir Henry lowered the lamp and he and Watson sat smoking cigarettes without making the least sound. One o'clock struck, and then two, and I felt they had almost given up in despair for the second time, when in an instant I sat bolt upright with all my senses keenly on the alert. I had heard the creak of a step in the passage. My sudden movement aroused the two men and they both turned to hear the steps stealthily pass along until they died away in the distance.

The baronet gently opened his door and we set out in pursuit. Already our man had gone round the gallery and the corridor was all in darkness. Softly we stole along until we had come into the other wing. We were just in time to catch a glimpse of the tall, black-bearded figure, his shoulders rounded as he tiptoed down the passage. Then he passed through the same door as before, and the light of the candle framed it in the darkness and shot one single yellow beam across the gloom of the corridor.

We shuffled cautiously towards it, trying every plank before we dared to put our whole weight upon it. The men had taken the precaution of leaving their boots behind us, but, even so, the old boards snapped and creaked beneath our tread. Sometimes it seemed impossible that he should fail to hear our approach. However, the man was fortunately rather deaf, and he entirely preoccupied in that which he was doing.

When at last we reached the door and peeped through, we found him crouching at the window, candle in hand, his white, intent face pressed against the pane, exactly as Watson and I had seen him two nights before.

We had arranged no plan of campaign, but it seems the baronet is a man to whom the most direct way is always the most natural. He walked into the room, and as he did so, Barrymore sprang up from the window with a sharp hiss of his breath and stood, livid and trembling, before us. His dark eyes, glaring out of the white mask of his face, were full of horror and astonishment as he gazed from Sir Henry to Watson and then to me, his eyes widening at the sight of a dog as part of this impromptu search party.

"What are you doing here, Barrymore?"

"Nothing, sir." His agitation was so great that he could hardly speak, and the shadows sprang up and down from the shaking of his candle. "It was the window, sir. I go round at night to see that they are fastened."

"On the second floor?"

"Yes, sir, all the windows."

"Look here, Barrymore," said Sir Henry sternly, "we have made up our minds to have the truth out of you, so it will save you trouble to tell it sooner rather than later. Come, now! No lies! What were you doing at that window?'

The fellow looked at us in a helpless way, and he wrung his

hands together like one who is in the last extremity of doubt and misery.

"I was doing no harm, sir. I was holding a candle to the window."

"And why were you holding a candle to the window?"

"Don't ask me, Sir Henry—don't ask me! I give you my word, sir, that it is not my secret, and that I cannot tell it. If it concerned no one but myself I would not try to keep it from you."

A sudden idea occurred to Watson, and he took the candle from the trembling hand of the butler.

"He must have been holding it as a signal," said Watson. "Let us see if there is any answer."

He held it as Barrymore had done, and stared out into the darkness. Vaguely we could discern the black bank of the trees and the lighter expanse of the moor, for the moon was behind the clouds. And then Watson gave a cry of exultation, for a tiny pinpoint of yellow light had suddenly transfixed the dark veil, and glowed steadily in the center of the black square framed by the window.

"There it is!" he cried.

"No, no, sir, it is nothing—nothing at all!" the butler broke in; "I assure you, sir—"

"Move your light across the window, Watson!" cried the baronet. "See, the other moves also! Now, you rascal, do you deny that it is a signal? Come, speak up! Who is your confederate out yonder, and what is this conspiracy that is going on?"

The man's face became openly defiant. "It is my business, and not yours. I will not tell."

"Then you leave my employment right away."

"Very good, sir. If I must, I must."

"And you go in disgrace. By thunder, you may well be ashamed of yourself. Your family has lived with mine for over a hundred years under this roof, and here I find you deep in some dark plot against me."

"No, no, sir; no, not against you!"

It was a woman's voice who said that last. Mrs. Barrymore, paler and more horrorstruck than her husband, was standing at the door.

"We have to go, Eliza. This is the end of it. You can pack our things," said the butler.

"Oh, John, John, have I brought you to this? It is my doing, Sir Henry—all mine. He has done nothing except for my sake and because I asked him."

"Speak out, then! What does it mean?"

"My unhappy brother is starving on the moor. We cannot let him perish at our very gates. The light is a signal to him that food is ready for him, and his light out yonder is to show the spot to which to bring it."

"Then your brother is—"

"The escaped convict, sir—Selden, the criminal," said she with a slight hitch in her voice. "My name was Selden, and he is my younger brother. We humored him too much when he was a lad and as he grew older he met wicked companions, and the devil entered into him until he broke my mother's heart and dragged our name in the dirt. But to me, sir, he was always the little curly-headed boy that I had nursed and played with as an elder sister would."

Her husband continued her tale. "That was why he broke prison, sir. He knew that she was here and that she could not refuse to help him. When he dragged himself here one night, weary and starving, with the warders hard at his heels, what could we do? We took him in and fed him and cared for him."

"Then you returned, sir," his wife continued. "And my brother thought he would be safer on the moor than anywhere else until the hue and cry was over, so he lay in hiding there. But every second night we made sure if he was still there by putting a light in the window, and, if there was an answer, my husband took out some bread and meat to him. Every day we hoped that he was gone, but as long as he was there we could not desert him. That is the whole truth, as I am an honest Christian woman and you will see that if there is blame in the matter it does not lie with my husband but with me, for whose sake he has done all that he has."

The woman's words came with an intense earnestness which carried conviction with them.

"Is this true, Barrymore?"

"Yes, Sir Henry. Every word of it."

"Well, I cannot blame you for standing by your own wife. Forget what I have said. Go to your room, you two, and we shall talk further about this matter in the morning."

When they were gone, we looked out of the window again. Sir Henry had flung it open, and the cold night wind beat in upon our faces. Far away in the black distance there still glowed that one tiny point of yellow light.

"How far do you think it is?" asked Sir Henry.

"Not more than a mile or two off."

"Well, it cannot be far if Barrymore had to carry out the food to it. And he is waiting, this villain, beside that candle. By thunder, Watson, I am going out to take that man!"

"We will come with you," said Watson with a glance in my direction.

"Then get your revolver and put on your boots. The sooner we start the better, as the fellow may put out his light and be off."

CHAPTER 10

*I*n five minutes we were outside the door, starting upon our expedition. We hurried through the dark shrub-bery, amid the dull moaning of the autumn wind and the rustle of the falling leaves. The night air was heavy with the smell of damp and decay. Now and again the moon peeped out for an instant, but clouds were driving over the face of the sky, and just as we came out on the moor a thin rain began to fall. The light still burned steadily ahead of us.

"Are you armed?" Watson asked.

"I have a hunting-crop."

"We must close in on him rapidly, for he is said to be a desperate fellow. We shall take him by surprise and have him at our mercy before he can resist."

"I say, Watson," said the baronet, "what would Holmes say to this? How about that hour of darkness in which the power of evil is exalted?"

As if in answer to his words, there rose suddenly out of the vast gloom of the moor that strange cry which Watson and I had already heard upon the borders of the great Grimpen Mire. It came with the wind through the silence of the night, a long, deep mutter then a rising howl, and then the sad moan in which it died away. Again and again it sounded, the whole air throbbing with it, strident, wild, and menacing. The baronet caught Watson's sleeve and his face glimmered white through the darkness.

"My God, what's that, Watson?"

Watson looked to me, as if my face would provide the answer he sought. In all honesty, my ears could not identify the sound. If its source was in fact canine, it was a strain of which I had no acquaintance.

"I don't know. It's a sound they have on the moor. I heard it once before." It died away, and an absolute silence closed in upon us. I cocked one ear and then the other, with no improvement. The true nature of the sound was beyond my ken.

"Watson," said the baronet, "it was the cry of a hound."

There was a break in his voice which told of the sudden horror which had seized him.

"What do they call this sound?" he asked.

"Who?"

"The folk on the countryside."

"Oh, they are ignorant people. Why should you mind what they call it?"

"Tell me, Watson. What do they say of it?"

Watson hesitated but could not escape the question.

"They say it is the cry of the Hound of the Baskervilles."

He groaned and was silent for a few moments.

"A hound it was," he said at last, "but it seemed to come from miles away, over yonder, I think."

"It was hard to say from where it came."

"It rose and fell with the wind. Isn't that the direction of the great Grimpen Mire?"

"Yes, it is."

"Well, it was up there. Come now, Watson, didn't you think yourself that it was the cry of a hound? I am not a child. You need not fear to speak the truth."

"Stapleton was with us when we heard it last. He said that it might be the calling of a strange bird."

"No, no, it was a hound. My God, can there be some truth in all these stories? Is it possible that I am really in danger from so dark a cause? You don't believe it, do you, Watson?"

"No, no."

"And yet it was one thing to laugh about it in London, and it is another to stand out here in the darkness of the moor and to hear such a cry as that. And my uncle! There was the footprint of the hound beside him as he lay. It all fits together. I don't think that I am a coward, Watson, but that sound seemed to freeze my very blood!"

"Shall we turn back?"

"No, by thunder; we have come out to get our man, and we will do it. We are after the convict, and a hell-hound, as likely as not, is after us. Come on! We'll see it through if all the fiends of the pit were loose upon the moor."

We stumbled slowly along in the darkness, with the black loom of the craggy hills around us, and the yellow speck of light burning steadily in front.

There is nothing so deceptive as the distance of a light upon a pitch-dark night, and sometimes the glimmer seemed to be far away upon the horizon and sometimes it might have been within a few yards of us. But at last we could see from where it came, and then we knew that we were indeed very close.

A candle was stuck in a crevice of the rocks which flanked it on each side, so as to keep the wind from it and also to prevent it from being visible, except in the direction of Baskerville Hall. A boulder of granite concealed our approach, and crouching behind it, we gazed over at the signal light. It was strange to see this single candle burning there in the middle of the moor, with no signs of life near it.

"What shall we do now?" whispered Sir Henry.

"Wait here. He must be near his light. Let us see if we can get a glimpse of him."

The words were hardly out of his mouth when we saw him. Over the rocks, in the crevice where the candle burned, there was thrust out an evil yellow face, a terrible animal face. Foul with mire, with a bristling beard, and hung with matted hair, the light beneath him was reflected in his small, cunning eyes.

Something had evidently aroused his suspicions. It may have been that Barrymore had some private signal which we had neglected to give, or the fellow may have had some other reason for thinking that all was not well, but I could read his fears upon his wicked face and his fear in the rank air.

Any instant he might dash out the light and vanish in the darkness. I sprang forward therefore, and Watson and Sir Henry did the same. At the same moment the convict screamed out a curse at us and hurled a rock which splintered up against the boulder which had sheltered us.

I caught one glimpse of his short, squat, strongly built figure as he sprang to his feet and turned to run. At the same moment by a lucky chance the moon broke through the clouds. We rushed over the brow of the hill, and there was our man running with great speed down the other side, springing over the stones with the skill of a mountain goat.

I was the fastest runner of the trio, but I soon found I had no chance of overtaking him. On a flat field he would have been mine in an instant, but my legs were not built for navigating the uneven, wet rocks.

We saw him for a long time in the moonlight until he was only a small speck moving swiftly among the boulders upon the side of a distant hill. I ran and ran, scrambling over the jutting rocks until I was completely winded, but the space between us grew ever wider. Finally I stopped and stood panting as Watson and Sir Henry caught up with me. We watched him disappearing into the distance.

And it was at this moment that there occurred a most strange and unexpected thing. We were turning to go home, having abandoned the hopeless chase. The moon was low upon the right and there, outlined as black as an ebony statue on that shining background, I saw the figure of a man upon the rocky peak.

He stood with his legs a little separated, his arms folded, his head bowed, as if he were brooding over that enormous wilderness of peat and granite which lay before him. It was not the convict. This man was far from the place where the latter had disappeared. Besides, he was a much taller man.

With a cry of surprise, Watson pointed him out to the baronet, but in the instant during which he had turned to grasp his arm, the man was gone. There was the sharp pinnacle of granite still cutting the lower edge of the moon, but its peak bore no trace of that silent and motionless figure.

I looked to Watson's face, to see what he had perceived in the short time he looked upon the man, but he gave no indication of anything other than shock.

"A prison guard, no doubt," said Watson. "The moor has been thick with them since this fellow escaped."

Sir Henry nodded in agreement and the two men once again began the slow trek back to Baskerville Hall. I lingered behind them for a long moment, looking at where the man had stood.

Watson had no doubt it had been a prison guard.

For my part, I did not share that opinion.

CHAPTER 11

The next morning we had a small scene after breakfast. Barrymore asked to speak with Sir Henry, and they were closeted in his study some little time.

Sitting with Watson in the billiard-room, I more than once heard the sound of voices raised, and I had a pretty good idea what point was under discussion. Watson, who feigned at reading the morning's paper, looked up at the same sounds I was hearing and we exchanged a mute look of understanding between us.

After a time the baronet opened his door and called for Watson. I followed on his heels.

"Barrymore considers that he has a grievance," he said. "He thinks that it was unfair on our part to hunt his brother-in-law down when he, of his own free will, had told us the secret."

The butler was standing very pale but very collected before us.

"I may have spoken too warmly, sir," said he. "And if I have, I am sure that I beg your pardon. At the same time, I was very much surprised when I heard you come back this morning and learned that you had been chasing Selden. The poor fellow has enough to fight against without my putting more upon his track."

"If you had told us of your own free will it would have been a different thing," said the baronet. "You only told us, or rather your wife only told us, when it was forced from you and you could not help yourself."

"I didn't think you would have taken advantage of it, Sir Henry — indeed I didn't."

"The man is a public danger. You only want to get a glimpse of his face to see that. Look at Mr. Stapleton's house, for example, with no one but himself to defend it."

"He will never trouble anyone in this country again. I assure you, Sir Henry, that in a very few days the necessary arrangements will have been made and he will be on his way to South America. For God's sake, sir, I beg of you not to let the police know that he is still on the moor. They have given up the chase there, and he can lie quiet until the ship is ready for him."

"But how about the chance of his holding someone up before he goes?"

"He would not do anything so mad, sir. We have provided him with all that he can want. To commit a crime would be to show where he was hiding."

"That is true," said Sir Henry. "Well, Barrymore—"

"God bless you, sir, and thank you from my heart! It would have killed my poor wife had he been taken again."

With a few broken words of gratitude the man turned, but he hesitated and then came back.

"You've been so kind to us, sir, that I should like to do the best I can do for you in return. I know something, Sir Henry, and perhaps I should have said it before, but it was long after the inquest that I found it out. I've never breathed a word about it yet to mortal man. It's about poor Sir Charles's death."

The baronet and Watson were both upon their feet. My attention, which had been waning, returned in full flower.

"Do you know how he died?" asked Sir Henry.

"No, sir, I don't know that."

"What then?"

"I know why he was at the gate at that hour. It was to meet a woman."

"To meet a woman! He?"

"Yes, sir."

"And the woman's name?"

"I can't give you the name, sir, but I can give you the initials. Her initials were L. L."

"How do you know this, Barrymore?"

"Well, Sir Henry, your uncle had a letter that morning. He had usually a great many letters, but that morning, as it chanced, there was only this one letter, so I took more notice of it. It was from Coombe Tracey, and it was addressed in a woman's hand."

"Well?"

"Well, sir, I thought no more of the matter, and never would have done had it not been for my wife. Only a few weeks ago she was cleaning out Sir Charles's study—it had never been touched since his death—and she found the ashes of a burned letter in the back of the grate. The greater part of it was charred to pieces, but one little slip, the end of a page, hung together, and the writing could still be read. It seemed to us to be a postscript at the end of the letter and it said: 'Please, please, as you are a gentleman, burn this letter, and be at the gate by ten o clock.' Beneath it were signed the initials L. L."

"Have you got that slip?"

"No, sir, it crumbled all to bits after we moved it."

"And you have no idea who L. L. is?"

"No, sir. No more than you have. But I expect if we could lay our hands upon that lady, we should know more about Sir Charles's death."

"I cannot understand, Barrymore, how you came to conceal this important information."

"Well, sir, we were both of us very fond of Sir Charles, as we well might be, considering all that he has done for us. To rake this up couldn't help our poor master."

"You thought it might injure his reputation?"

"Well, sir, I thought no good could come of it."

"Very good, Barrymore; you can go."

When the butler had left us, Sir Henry turned to Watson. "Well, Watson, what do you think of this new light?"

"It seems to leave the darkness rather blacker than before."

"I agree. But if we can only trace L. L., it should clear up the whole business. We have gained that much. We know that there is someone who has the facts if we can only find her. What do you think we should do?"

"Let Holmes know all about it at once. It might give him the clue for which he has been seeking. I am much mistaken if it does not bring him down."

* * *

THE NEXT DAY THE RAIN POURED DOWN, RUSTLING ON THE IVY AND dripping from the eaves. I thought of the convict out upon the bleak, cold, shelterless moor. Poor devil! Whatever his crimes, he had suffered something fierce to atone for them.

In the evening, the rain subsided. As the sun was setting behind the clouds, I approached Watson, and dropped my leash at his feet. He took pity upon me and, pulling on his coat, we headed toward the door. Mrs. Hudson had sewn for me a Macintosh of my own, but that was back in London, which was fine by me, as I was no fan of wearing the silly thing. There was a chill in the air, but it was a fresh breeze which greeted us, far unlike the normal fetid damp of the wet moorland.

We walked far upon the sodden moor, full of dark imaginings, the wind whistling about my ears. God help those who wander into the great mire now, for even the firm uplands are becoming a morass.

After a walk of a half-hours' time, in the distance the two thin towers of Baskerville Hall rose above the trees. They were the only signs of human life which I could see. Nowhere was there any trace of that man whom I had recognized on the same spot two nights before.

As we walked back, we were overtaken by Dr. Mortimer driving in his dog-cart. He had been very attentive to us, and hardly a day had passed that he had not called at the Hall to see how we were getting on.

He insisted upon us climbing into his dog-cart, and he gave us a lift homeward.

"By the way, Mortimer," said Watson as we jolted along the rough road, "I suppose there are few people living within driving distance whom you do not know?"

"Hardly any I think."

"Can you, then, tell me the name of any woman whose initials are L. L.?"

He thought for a few minutes.

"No," said he. "There are a few laboring folk for whom I can't answer, but among the farmers or gentry there is no one whose initials are those. Wait a bit though," he added after a pause. "There is Laura Lyons—her initials are L. L.—but she lives in Coombe Tracey."

"Who is she?" Watson asked.

"She is Frankland's daughter."

"What! Old Frankland the crank?"

"Exactly. She married an artist named Lyons, who came sketching on the moor. He proved to be a blackguard and deserted her. Her father refused to have anything to do with her because she had married without his consent and perhaps for one or two other reasons as well. So, between the old sinner and the young one, the girl has had a pretty bad time."

"How does she live?"

"I fancy old Frankland allows her a pittance, but it cannot be more, for his own affairs are considerably involved. Her story got about, and several of the people here did something to enable her to earn an honest living. Stapleton did for one, and Sir Charles for another. I gave a trifle myself. It was to set her up in a typewriting business."

I could see Watson was filing this information and I had little doubt that on the morrow we would find our way to Coombe Tracey to see this Mrs. Laura Lyons.

* * *

Dr. Mortimer stayed to dinner, and he and the baronet played Ecarte afterwards, a game with which I was unfamiliar. After a hand or two I perceived the point of the play and retired myself to the library and settled myself in front of the fire. While I can understand the concept of playing cards, the observation of the same holds little appeal when one is a non-participant.

Watson must have felt the same way, as he was in the library ahead of me, working on one of his long letters to Holmes. The butler brought him some coffee, and Watson took the moment to ask him a few questions.

"Well," said Watson, "has this precious relation of yours departed, or is he still lurking out yonder?"

"I don't know, sir. I hope to heaven that he has gone, for he has brought nothing but trouble here! I've not heard of him since I left out food for him last, and that was three days ago."

"Did you see him then?"

"No, sir, but the food was gone when next I went that way."

"Then he was certainly there?"

"So you would think, sir, unless it was the other man who took it."

Watson sat with his coffee—cup halfway to his lips—and stared at Barrymore.

"You know that there is another man then?"

"Yes, sir; there is another man upon the moor."

"Have you seen him?"

"No, sir."

"How do you know of him then?"

"Selden told me of him, sir, a week ago or more. He's in hiding, too, but he's not a convict as far as I can make out. I don't like it, Dr. Watson—I tell you straight, sir, that I don't like it." He spoke with a sudden passion of earnestness.

"Tell me, frankly, what it is that you don't like."

Barrymore hesitated for a moment, as if he regretted his outburst or found it difficult to express his own feelings in words.

"It's all these goings-on, sir," he cried at last, waving his hand towards the rain-lashed window which faced the moor. "There's foul play somewhere, and there's black villainy brewing, to that I'll swear! Very glad I should be, sir, to see Sir Henry on his way back to London again!"

"But what is it that alarms you?"

"Look at Sir Charles's death! Look at the noises on the moor at night. There's not a man would cross it after sundown if he was paid for it. Look at this stranger hiding out yonder, and watching and waiting! What's he waiting for? What does it mean? It means no good to anyone of the name of Baskerville. And very glad I shall be to be quit of it all on the day that Sir Henry's new servants are ready to take over the Hall."

"But about this stranger," persisted Watson. "What did Selden say?"

"At first he thought that he was the police, but soon he found that he had some problem of his own."

"And where did he say that he lived?"

"Among the old houses on the hillside—the stone huts where the old folk used to live."

"But how about his food?"

"Selden found out that he has got a lad who works for him and brings all he needs. I dare say he goes to Coombe Tracey for what he wants."

"Very good, Barrymore. We may talk further of this some other time."

When the butler had gone, Watson walked over to the window and looked through a blurred pane at the driving clouds and at the tossing outline of the wind-swept trees. I knew he was parsing the details of the last days' events, trying to employ the tricks Holmes had taught us both.

I felt I had Watson at an unfair advantage in this singular situation, but could think of no way to make him wiser in this moment. As he continued to stare out the window, I got up, adjusted my position ever so slightly, and lay back down in front of the fire.

CHAPTER 12

*W*atson had no opportunity to tell the baronet what we had learned about Mrs. Lyons upon the evening before, for Dr. Mortimer remained with him at cards until it was very late. At breakfast, however, Watson informed him about the discovery and asked him whether he would care to accompany us to Coombe Tracey.

At first Sir Henry was very eager to come, but on second thought it was decided if we went without him, the results might be more productive. The more formal we made the visit, the less information we might obtain.

So we left Sir Henry behind, and Perkins drove us off in the open carriage upon our new quest.

When we reached Coombe Tracey, Watson told Perkins to put up the horses. A maid showed us in without ceremony, and as we entered the sitting-room, a lady who was sitting before a Remington typewriter, sprang up with a pleasant smile of welcome.

"Well, who is this fine fellow?" she asked, moving quickly toward us. At the last moment, she dropped down upon one knee and gave the top of my head a well-appreciated pet. I leaned into the action and she kindly scratched behind each of my ears. She then looked up at Watson and her expression changed to one of deep concern.

"And who might you be?" she asked.

"I have the pleasure," said Watson, "of knowing your father."

It was a clumsy introduction, and the lady made no effort to hide her reaction to it.

"There is nothing in common between my father and me," she said. "I owe him nothing, and his friends are not mine. If it were not for the late Sir Charles Baskerville and some other kind hearts, I might have starved for all that my father cared."

"It was about the late Sir Charles Baskerville that I have come here to see you."

"And you are?"

"Dr. John Watson, a friend of the current baronet."

"And who is this fine fellow?" she asked, once again turning her attention to me.

"Ah, this is Septimus," said Watson haltingly. "He is companion to a friend of mine, and he has joined me here during my stay at Baskerville Hall."

"Septimus," she repeated, running her hand along the length of my back. "From a litter of at least seven, am I to assume?"

"That has always been my understanding," lied Watson. "As I mentioned, he belongs to my friend."

In point of fact, Holmes has never landed on a solid explanation of his naming choice for me. I know my mother birthed a large litter of nine, but there is no actual way to determine my birth order. On one occasion, Holmes claimed I was named for a Roman emperor; on other occasions, he has claimed I was named for characters in *The Moonstone* or *The Mystery of Edwin Drood*. However, since Holmes never, to my knowledge, read fiction in my presence, I strongly doubt these last two options. If pressed, I would say he liked the sound of the name and leave it at that.

"What can I tell you about Sir Charles?" she asked coolly as she crossed the room, returning to her typewriter.

"You knew him, did you not?"

"I have already said that I owe a great deal to his kindness. If I am able to support myself it is largely due to the interest which he took in my unhappy situation."

"Did you correspond with him?"

The lady looked up quickly with an angry gleam in her eyes.

"What is the object of your questions?" she asked sharply.

"The object is to avoid a public scandal. It is better that I should ask them here than that the matter should pass outside our control."

She was silent and her face was still very pale. At last she looked up.

"I certainly wrote to him once or twice to acknowledge his generosity."

"Have you ever met him?"

"Yes, once or twice, when he came into Coombe Tracey. He was a very retiring man, and he preferred to do good by stealth."

"But if you saw him so seldom and wrote so seldom, how did he know enough about your affairs to be able to help you, as you say that he has done?"

She met this question with the utmost readiness.

"There were several gentlemen who knew my sad history and united to help me. One was Mr. Stapleton, a neighbor and intimate friend of Sir Charles's. He was exceedingly kind, and it was through him that Sir Charles learned about my troubles."

"Did you ever write to Sir Charles asking him to meet you?" Watson continued.

Mrs. Lyons flushed with anger again. "Really, sir, this is a very extraordinary question."

"I am sorry, madam, but I must repeat it."

"Then I answer, certainly not."

"Not on the very day of Sir Charles's death?"

The flush had faded in an instant, and a deathly face was before me. Her dry lips could not speak the "No" which I saw rather than heard.

"Surely your memory deceives you," said Watson. "I could even quote a passage of your letter. It ran 'Please, please, as you are a gentleman, burn this letter, and be at the gate by ten o'clock.'"

She swooned a bit and I thought that she had fainted, but she recovered herself by a supreme effort.

"Is there no such thing as a gentleman?" she gasped.

"You do Sir Charles an injustice. He did burn the letter. But sometimes a letter may be legible even when burned. You acknowledge now that you wrote it?"

"Yes, I did write it," she cried, pouring out her soul in a torrent of words. "I did write it. Why should I deny it? I have no reason to be ashamed of it. I wished him to help me. I believed that if I had an interview I could gain his help, so I asked him to meet me."

"But why at such an hour?"

"Because I had only just learned that he was going to London the next day and might be away for months. There were reasons why I could not get there earlier."

"But why a rendezvous in the garden instead of a visit to the house?"

"Do you think a woman could go alone at that hour to a bachelor's house?"

"Well, what happened when you did get there?"

"I never went."

"Mrs. Lyons!"

"No, I swear it to you on all I hold sacred. I never went. Something intervened to prevent my going."

"What was that?"

"That is a private matter. I cannot tell it."

"You acknowledge then that you made an appointment with Sir Charles at the very hour and place at which he met his death, but you deny that you kept the appointment?"

"That is the truth."

"And why were you so pressing that Sir Charles should destroy your letter?"

"If you have read the letter you will know."

"I did not say that I had read all the letter."

"You quoted some of it."

"I quoted the postscript. The letter had, as I said, been burned and it was not all legible. I ask you once again why it was you were so concerned Sir Charles should destroy this letter which he received on the day of his death."

"The matter is a very private one."

"The more reason why you should avoid a public investigation."

"I will tell you, then. If you have heard anything of my unhappy history you will know that I made a rash marriage and had reason to regret it."

"I have heard as much."

"My life has been one incessant persecution from a husband whom I abhor. The law is upon his side, and every day I am faced by the possibility that he may force me to live with him. At the time that I wrote this letter to Sir Charles, I had learned that there was a prospect of my regaining my freedom if certain expenses could be met. I knew Sir Charles's generosity, and I thought that if he heard the story from my own lips he would help me."

"Then how is it that you did not go?"

"Because I received help in the interval from another source."

"Why then, did you not write to Sir Charles and explain this?"

"I would have done so, had I not seen his death announced in the paper the next morning."

From my perspective, the woman's story hung coherently together, and all of Watson's questions were unable to shake it.

After a few more comments, she bade us goodbye, offering a much warmer farewell to me than was given to poor Watson.

* * *

DURING THE JOURNEY BACK TOWARD BASKERVILLE, I COULD SEE that Watson was puzzling his next step. He peered constantly toward the moor and the prehistoric huts which spanned its length and breath. I sensed that would be our next destination, as I knew he was still haunted by the figure of the man we had witnessed with Sir Henry that other evening.

Luck had been against us again and again in this inquiry, but now at last it came to our aid. And the messenger of good fortune was none other than Mr. Frankland, who was standing, gray-whiskered and red-faced, outside the gate of his garden, which opened on to the highroad along which we travelled.

"Good-day, Dr. Watson," cried he with odd good humor. "You must really give your horses a rest and come in to have a glass of wine and to congratulate me."

I could tell Watson was anxious to send Perkins and the wagonette home because this opportunity was a good one. We alighted and Watson sent a message to Sir Henry that we should walk over in time for dinner. Then we followed Frankland into his dining-room.

"It is a great day for me, sir—one of the red-letter days of my life," he cried with many chuckles. "I have brought off a double event. These infernal people seem to think that there are no rights of property, and that they can swarm where they like. Both cases decided Dr. Watson, and both in my favor. I haven't had such a day since I had Sir John Morland for trespass because he shot in his own warren."

"How on earth did you do that?"

"Look it up in the books, sir. It will repay reading—Frankland v. Morland, Court of Queen's Bench. It cost me 200 pounds, but I got my verdict."

"Did it do you any good?"

"None, sir, none. I am proud to say that I had no interest in the matter. And I will say this: were I treated more fairly by my neighbors, I would happily offer them what they are dying to know; but nothing would induce me to help the rascals in any way."

"Some poaching case, no doubt?" said Watson with an indifferent manner.

"Ha, ha, my boy, a very much more important matter than that! What about the convict on the moor?"

Watson stared. "You don't mean that you know where he is?" said he.

"I may not know exactly where he is, but I am quite sure that I could help the police to lay their hands on him. Has it never struck you that the way to catch that man was to find out where he got his food and so trace it to him?"

That struck me an idea which was getting uncomfortably near the truth.

"No doubt," said Watson. "But how do you know that he is anywhere upon the moor?"

"I know it because I have seen with my own eyes the messenger who takes him his food."

I knew Watson's thoughts immediately went to Barrymore. But the old man's next remark took a weight from his mind.

"You'll be surprised to hear that his food is taken to him by a child. I see him every day through my telescope upon the roof. He passes along the same path at the same hour, and to whom should he be going except to the convict?"

"I should say that it was much more likely that it was the son of one of the moorland shepherds taking out his father's dinner."

The appearance of opposition seemed to strike fire in of the old man. His eyes looked malignantly at Watson, and his gray whiskers bristled like those of an angry cat.

"Indeed, sir!" said he, pointing out over the wide-stretching moor. "Do you see that rocky peak over yonder? Well, do you see the low hill beyond? It is the stoniest part of the whole moor. Is that a place where a shepherd would be likely to take his station? Your suggestion, sir, is a most absurd one."

Watson meekly answered that he had spoken without knowing all the facts. This submission pleased the old man and led him to further confidences.

"You may be sure, sir, that I have seen the boy again and again with his bundle. Every day, and sometimes twice a day, I have been able—but wait a moment, Dr. Watson. Do my eyes deceive me, or is there at the present moment something moving upon that hillside?"

It was several miles off, but I could distinctly see a small dark dot against the dull green and gray, which I recognized as the figure of a young boy. The humans, with their lesser eyesight, turned immediately to mechanical means to achieve the same effect.

"Come, sir, come!" cried Frankland, rushing upstairs. "You will see with your own eyes and judge for yourself."

The telescope, a formidable instrument mounted upon a tripod, stood upon the flat roof of the house. Frankland clapped his eye to it and gave a cry of satisfaction.

"Quick, Dr. Watson, quick, before he passes over the hill!"

As they studied him through the glass, I saw without such aid as he reached the crest. Then he vanished over the hill.

"Well! Am I right?" cried the old man.

"Certainly, there is a boy who seems to have some secret errand," agreed Watson.

"And what the errand is even a county constable could guess. But not one word shall they have from me, and I bind you to secrecy also, Dr. Watson. Not a word! You understand!"

"Just as you wish."

"Nothing would induce me to help the police in any way. Surely you are not going! You will help me to empty the decanter in honor of this great occasion!"

But Watson, wisely, resisted all his solicitations and succeeded in dissuading him from his announced intention of walking home with us.

We kept to the road as long as his eye was on us, and then we struck off across the moor and made for the stony hill over which the boy had disappeared.

The sun was already sinking when we reached the summit of the hill. Over the wide expanse there was no sound and no movement. One great gray bird, a gull or curlew, soared aloft in the blue heaven. The three of us seemed to be the only living things between the huge arch of the sky and the desert beneath it.

The boy was nowhere to be seen, although I could smell him and of course his master. But I let Watson lead, in part because I was curious as to where his instincts would take us.

Down beneath a cleft of the hills there was a circle of the old stone huts, and in the middle of them there was one which retained sufficient roof to act as a screen against the weather.

"That must be the burrow where the stranger lurks," Watson whispered. "At last my foot is on the threshold of his hiding place —his secret is within our grasp."

As we approached the hut, Watson walked as warily as Stapleton would do when he drew near a settled butterfly with a poised net. A vague pathway among the boulders led to the dilapidated opening which served as a door. All was silent within.

Throwing aside his cigarette, Watson closed his hand upon the butt of his revolver and, walking swiftly up to the door, he looked in. As I could have told him, the place was empty.

But there were ample signs that we had not come upon a false scent. This was certainly where the man lived. Some blankets rolled in a waterproof lay upon the ground. The ashes of a fire were heaped in a rude grate. Beside it lay some cooking utensils and a bucket half-full of water. A litter of empty tins showed that the place had been occupied for some time.

In the middle of the hut a flat stone served the purpose of a table, and upon this stood a small cloth bundle—the same, no doubt, which I had seen upon the shoulder of the boy—and which Watson had spied through the telescope. He opened it, revealing that it contained a loaf of bread, a tinned tongue, and two tins of preserved peaches.

As he set it down again, after having examined it, Watson noticed that beneath it there lay a sheet of paper with writing upon it. He raised it and read aloud what was roughly scrawled in pencil: "Dr. Watson has gone to Coombe Tracey."

Watson puzzled over this for a long moment, even going so far as to read it aloud a second time.

"So it is I, then, and not Sir Henry, who is being dogged by this secret man," Watson said in almost a whisper. "He has not followed me himself, but he has set an agent—the boy, perhaps—upon my track, and this was his report. Possibly I had taken no step since I had been upon the moor which had not been observed and reported."

Watson then conducted a thorough search of the hut, to discover any sign which might indicate the character or intentions of the man who lived in this singular place. Had I the ability, I could have spared him the search, but since that was not an option I wandered outside.

The sun was sinking low and its reflection was shot back in ruddy patches by the distant pools which lay amid the great Grimpen Mire. There were the two towers of Baskerville Hall, and there a distant blur of smoke which marked the village of Grimpen. Between the two, behind the hill, was the house of the Stapletons.

All was peaceful in the golden evening light, and yet Watson continued his search, finally settling down in the dark recess of the hut while he waited with sombre patience for the coming of its tenant. I joined him and lay on the cold ground next to him, as he sat there, his eyes on the rough doorway while his revolver sat waiting in his hand.

And then at last I heard him, my ears perking to the sound. Far away came the sharp clink of a boot striking upon a stone, which Watson heard as well. Then another and yet another, coming nearer and nearer.

Watson shrank back into the darkest corner and cocked the pistol in his hand, while I took the opposite tack and moved toward the doorway in anticipation. I heard him swear softly at me to return, which I chose to not heed.

There was a long pause which showed that the man approaching had stopped. Then once more the footsteps approached and a shadow fell across the opening of the hut.

"Ah, Septimus, you anticipate me," said the well-known voice. "Here, I have hoarded a treat for you, in anticipation of your tracking me."

He tossed me the morsel and then turned to Watson. "It is a lovely evening, my dear Watson. I really think that you will be more comfortable outside than in."

CHAPTER 13

"*H*olmes!" Watson cried—"Holmes!"

"Come out," said he, "and please be careful with the revolver."

Watson stooped under the rude lintel and I followed directly. There he sat, upon a stone outside, his gray eyes dancing with amusement as they fell upon Watson's astonished features. He was thin and worn, but clear and alert, his keen face bronzed by the sun and roughened by the wind. He had contrived, with that catlike love of personal cleanliness which was one of his characteristics, that his chin should be as smooth and his linen as perfect as if he were in Baker Street.

"I never was more glad to see anyone in my life," said Watson as he wrung Holmes by the hand.

"Or more astonished, eh?" said Holmes, turning and giving me a wink. He knew his secret had been safe with me from the moment I recognized him on that rocky outcropping, silhouetted by the moon.

"Well, I must confess to it."

"The surprise was not all on one side, I assure you. I had no idea that you had found my occasional retreat, still less that you were inside it, until I was within twenty paces of the door."

"My footprint, I presume?"

"No, Watson. If you seriously desire to deceive me, you must change your tobacconist; for when I see the stub of a cigarette marked Bradley, Oxford Street, I know that my friend Watson is in the neighborhood. You will see it there beside the path. You threw it down, no doubt, at that supreme moment when you charged into the empty hut."

"Exactly."

"However, I did recognize a footprint. It was the print of your partner, the able Septimus," said Holmes, giving my head an uncharacteristically warm pat. "The gait of a greyhound, even on such rocky terrain, stands apart, even in this light." He turned back to Watson. "So, you actually thought that I was the criminal?"

"I did not know who you were, but I was determined to find out."

"Excellent, Watson! And how did you localize me? You saw me, perhaps, on the night of the convict hunt, when I was so imprudent as to allow the moon to rise behind me?"

"Yes, we saw you then."

"And have no doubt searched all the huts until you came to this one?"

"No, your boy had been observed, and that gave us a guide where to look."

"The old gentleman with the telescope, no doubt. I could not make it out when first I saw the light flashing upon the lens." He rose and peeped into the hut. "Ha, I see that Cartwright has brought up some supplies. What's this paper? So you have been to Coombe Tracey, have you?"

"Yes."

"To see Mrs. Laura Lyons?"

"Exactly."

"Well done! Our researches have evidently been running on parallel lines, and when we unite our results, I expect we shall have a fairly full knowledge of the case."

"But how in the name of wonder did you come here, and what have you been doing? I thought that you were in Baker Street working out that case of blackmailing."

"That was what I wished you to think."

"Then you use me, and yet do not trust me!" Watson cried with some bitterness. "I think that I have deserved better at your hands, Holmes. It seems even Septimus here had a better idea of the reality of our situation than I did!"

"My dear fellow, both you and Septimus have been invaluable to me—in your own, unique ways—in this as in many other cases. I beg that you will forgive me if I have seemed to play a trick upon you. As it is, I have been able to get about as I could not possibly have done had I been living in the Hall, and I remain an unknown factor in the business, ready to throw in all my weight at a critical moment."

"But why keep me in the dark?"

"For you to have been in the know could not have helped us and might possibly have led to my discovery. You would have wished to tell me something, or in your kindness you would have brought me out some comfort or other, and so an unnecessary risk would be run. I brought Cartwright down with me—you remember the little chap at the express office—and he has seen after my simple wants: a loaf of bread and a clean collar. What does man want more? He has also given me an extra pair of eyes upon a very active pair of feet, and both have been invaluable.

"And now," he continued, "tell me the result of your visit to Mrs. Laura Lyons—it was not difficult for me to guess that it was to see her that you had gone, for I am already aware that she is the one person in Coombe Tracey who might be of service to us in this matter. In fact, if you had not gone today, it is exceedingly probable that I should have gone tomorrow."

The sun had set and dusk was settling over the moor. The air had turned chill and we withdrew into the hut for warmth. There sitting together in the twilight, Watson told Holmes of our visit with the lady, glossing over the young woman's obvious affection for me. So interested was Holmes that Watson had to repeat some of it twice before he was satisfied.

"This is most important," said Holmes when Watson had concluded." It fills up a gap which I had been unable to bridge in this most complex affair. You are aware, perhaps, that a close intimacy exists between this lady and the man Stapleton?"

"I did not know of a close intimacy."

"There can be no doubt about the matter. They meet, they write, there is a complete understanding between them. Now, this puts a very powerful weapon into our hands. If I could only use it to detach his wife."

"His wife?"

"I am giving you some information now, in return for all that you have given me. The lady who has passed here as Miss Stapleton is in reality his wife."

"Good heavens, Holmes! Are you sure of what you say? How could he have permitted Sir Henry to fall in love with her?"

"Sir Henry's falling in love could do no harm to anyone except Sir Henry. I repeat that the lady is his wife and not his sister."

"But why this elaborate deception?"

"Because he foresaw that she would be very much more useful to him in the character of a free woman."

"It is he, then, who is our enemy—it is he who dogged us in London?"

"I do believe so," said Holmes.

"But are you sure of this, Holmes? How do you know that the woman is his wife?"

"He was once a schoolmaster in the north of England. Now, there is no one more easy to trace than a schoolmaster. A little investigation showed me that a school had come to grief under atrocious circumstances, and that the man who had owned it—the name was different—had disappeared with his wife. The descriptions agreed. When I learned that the missing man was devoted to entomology, the identification was complete."

"If this woman is in truth his wife, where does Mrs. Laura Lyons come in?" asked Watson.

"Your interview with the lady has cleared the situation very much. I did not know about a projected divorce between herself and her husband. In that case, regarding Stapleton as an unmarried man, she counted no doubt upon becoming his wife."

"And when she learns the truth?"

"Why, then we may find the lady to be of great service to us. It must be our first duty to see her tomorrow," said Holmes. He looked around at the dimming light, seeming to notice it for the first time. "Don't you think, Watson, that you are away from your charge rather long? Your place should be at Baskerville Hall."

The last red streaks had faded away in the west and night had settled upon the moor. A few faint stars were gleaming in a violet sky. And then, a terrible scream—a prolonged yell of horror and anguish—burst out of the silence of the moor. I must admit that the frightful cry turned the blood to ice in my veins.

"Oh, my God!" gasped Watson. "What is it? What does it mean?"

Like me, Holmes had sprung to his feet.

"Hush!" he whispered. "Hush!"

The cry had pealed out from somewhere far off on the shadowy plain. Now it burst upon our ears again, nearer, louder, more urgent than before.

"Where is it?" Holmes whispered; and I knew from the tone of his voice that he, the man of iron, was shaken to the soul. "Where is it?"

"There, I think." Watson pointed into the darkness.

"No, there!"

Again the agonized cry swept through the silent night, louder and much nearer than ever. And then a new sound mingled with it, a deep, muttered rumble, menacing, rising and falling.

"The hound!" cried Holmes. "Come, come! Great heavens, if we are too late!"

I started running swiftly over the moor, and the two men followed at my heels. But now from somewhere among the broken ground immediately in front of us there came one last despairing yell, and then a dull, heavy thud. We halted and listened. Not another sound broke the heavy silence of the windless night.

I saw Holmes put his hand to his forehead like a man distracted. He stamped his feet upon the ground.

"He has beaten us, Watson. We are too late."

"No, no, surely not!"

"Fool that I was to hold my hand. And you, Watson, see what comes of abandoning your charge! But, by Heaven, if the worst has happened we'll avenge him!"

Blindly we ran through the gloom, blundering against boulders, forcing our way through thorny bushes, panting up hills and rushing down slopes, heading always in the direction whence those dreadful sounds had come. At every rise, Holmes looked eagerly round him, but the shadows were thick upon the moor, and nothing moved upon its dreary face.

"Can you see anything?"

"Nothing."

"But, hark, what is that?"

A low moan had fallen upon my ears. There it was again upon my left! On that side a ridge of rocks ended in a sheer cliff which overlooked a stone-strewn slope. On its jagged face was spread-eagled some dark, irregular object.

As I raced towards it, the vague outline hardened into a definite shape. It was a prostrate man, face downward upon the ground, the head doubled under him at a horrible angle.

Not a whisper, not a rustle, rose now from the dark figure

over which I stooped. Holmes arrive seconds later and laid his hand upon the man, and then held it up again with an exclamation of horror. The gleam of the match which he struck shone upon his bloodied fingers and upon the ghastly pool which widened slowly from the crushed skull of the victim.

"It's Sir Henry Baskerville!" gasped Watson. "There is no chance of forgetting that peculiar ruddy tweed suit—the very one which he had worn on the first morning that we saw him in Baker Street."

Holmes groaned, and his face glimmered white through the darkness.

"The brute! The brute!" Watson cried with clenched hands. "Oh Holmes, I shall never forgive myself for having left him to his fate."

"I am more to blame than you, Watson. In order to have my case well rounded and complete, I have thrown away the life of my client. It is the greatest blow which has befallen me in my career."

I stepped forward and gave the body another, more thorough sniff, my mind racing. The smell was familiar, but strangely out of place.

"That we should have heard his screams—my God, those screams!—and yet have been unable to save him!" continued Watson. "Where is this brute of a hound which drove him to his death? It may be lurking among these rocks at this instant."

I turned to Holmes, but he was still caught up in more emotion than I have ever seen upon him.

"And Stapleton, where is he? He shall answer for this deed. By heavens, cunning as he is, the fellow shall be in my power before another day is past!"

I considered my options, which appeared to be few.

"Why should we not seize him at once?"

"Our case is not complete," explained Holmes. "The fellow is wary and cunning to the last degree. It is not what we know, but what we can prove. If we make one false move the villain may escape us yet."

With no other recourse, I barked.

It was a loud, sharp exclamation. The very sound of it made both men jump, if only slightly. Holmes looked down upon me, recognizing that this action—the delivery of a single, loud bark— was a rare occurrence indeed on my part. I moved again toward the prone figure, lowering myself and giving the body the slightest of nudges.

This was enough to stir Holmes into action. He knelt down upon the marshy land and gently rolled the body, oh so slightly but just enough so that for the first time he was able to get a clear look at the man's face.

He uttered a cry and jumped up, dancing and laughing, and then bent down and petted my head with such enthusiasm I was afraid he might create a lasting bruise.

"Oh, Septimus, my boy, you have come through yet again!" he declared. He then looked up at Watson. "A beard! A beard! The man has a beard!"

"A beard?"

"It is not the baronet—it is—why, it is my neighbor, the convict!"

With feverish haste they had turned the body over, and that dripping beard was pointing up to the cold, clear moon. There could be no doubt about the thick forehead, the sunken animal eyes. It was indeed the same face which had glared upon us in the light of the candle from over the rock—the face of Selden, the criminal.

"The baronet told me that he had handed his old wardrobe to Barrymore," said Watson quickly. "Barrymore passed it on in order to help Selden in his escape. Boots, shirt, cap—it was all Sir Henry's."

"Then the clothes have been the poor devil's death," said Holmes. "It is clear enough that the hound has been laid on from some article of Sir Henry's—the boot which was abstracted in the hotel, in all probability—and so ran this man down. There is one very singular thing, however: How came Selden, in the darkness, to know that the hound was on his trail?"

"He heard him."

"To hear a hound upon the moor would not work a hard man like this convict into such a paroxysm of terror that he would risk recapture by screaming wildly for help. By his cries he must have run a long way after he knew the animal was on his track. How did he know?"

"A greater mystery to me is why this hound, presuming that all our conjectures are correct—"

"I presume nothing."

"Well, then, why this hound should be loose tonight. I suppose that it does not always run loose upon the moor. Stapleton would not let it go unless he had reason to think that Sir Henry would be there."

"Halloa, Watson, what's this?" said Holmes, peering into the murk. "It's the man himself, by all that's wonderful and audacious! Not a word to show our suspicions—not a word, or my plans crumble to the ground."

A figure was approaching us over the moor, and I saw the dull red glow of a cigar. The moon shone upon him, and I could distinguish the dapper shape and jaunty walk of the naturalist. He stopped when he saw us.

"Why, Dr. Watson, that's not you, is it? You are the last man that I should have expected to see out on the moor at this time of night. But, dear me, what's this? Somebody hurt? Not—don't tell me that it is our friend Sir Henry!" He hurried past me and stooped over the dead man. I heard a sharp intake of his breath and the cigar fell from his fingers.

"Who—who's this?" he stammered.

"It is Selden, the man who escaped from Princetown."

Stapleton turned a ghastly face upon us, but by a supreme

effort he had overcome his amazement and his disappointment. He looked sharply from Holmes to Watson, sparing not a second on me. "Dear me! What a very shocking affair! How did he die?"

"He appears to have broken his neck by falling over these rocks. My friend and I were strolling on the moor when we heard a cry."

"I heard a cry also. That was what brought me out. I was uneasy about Sir Henry."

"Why about Sir Henry in particular?"

"Because I had suggested that he should come over. When he did not come I was surprised, and I naturally became alarmed for his safety when I heard cries upon the moor. By the way"—his eyes darted again from Watson's face to Holmes's—"did you hear anything else besides a cry?"

"No," said Holmes. "Did you?"

"No."

"What do you mean, then?"

"Oh, you know the stories that the peasants tell about a phantom hound. It is said to be heard at night upon the moor. I was wondering if there were any evidence of such a sound tonight."

"We heard nothing of the kind," lied Watson. He acted the part perfectly, to the point that I came close myself to believing him.

"And what is your theory of this poor fellow's death?"

"I have no doubt that anxiety and exposure have driven him off his head," said Watson. "He has rushed about the moor in a crazy state and eventually fallen over here and broken his neck."

"That seems the most reasonable theory," said Stapleton, and he gave a sigh which I took to indicate his relief. "What do you think about it, Mr. Sherlock Holmes?"

My master bowed his compliments. "You are quick at identification," said he.

"We have been expecting you in these parts since Dr. Watson came down. You are in time to see a tragedy."

"Yes, indeed. I have no doubt that my friend's explanation will cover the facts. I will take an unpleasant remembrance back to London with me tomorrow."

"Oh, you return tomorrow?"

"That is my intention."

"I hope your visit has cast some light upon those occurrences which have puzzled us?"

Holmes shrugged his shoulders.

"One cannot always have the success for which one hopes. An investigator needs facts and not legends or rumors. It has not been a satisfactory case."

Holmes spoke in his frankest and most unconcerned manner. Stapleton still looked hard at him. Then he turned to Watson.

"I would suggest carrying this poor fellow to my house, but it would give my sister such a fright that I do not feel justified in doing it. I think that if we put something over his face he will be safe until morning."

And so it was arranged. Resisting Stapleton's offer of hospitality, Holmes, Watson and I set off to Baskerville Hall, leaving the naturalist to return alone.

Looking back, I saw his figure moving slowly away over the broad moor. It might have been a trick of the light, but for the briefest of seconds, it appeared that he turned and gave our group one final, furtive look.

And then he was gone.

CHAPTER 14

"What a nerve that fellow has!" said Holmes as we walked together across the moor. "How he pulled himself together in the face of what must have been a paralyzing shock when he found that the wrong man had fallen victim to his plot. I told you in London, and I tell you now again, that we have never had a foe more worthy of our steel."

"What effect do you think it will have upon his plans now that he knows you are here?"

"It may cause him to be more cautious, or it may drive him to immediate desperate measures. Like most clever criminals, he may be too confident in his own cleverness and imagine that he has completely deceived us."

"Why should we not arrest him at once?"

"My dear Watson, you were born to be a man of action. Your instinct is always to do something energetic. But supposing, for argument's sake, that we had him arrested tonight, what on earth the better off should we be for that? We could prove nothing against him."

"Surely we have a case."

"Not a shadow of one—only surmise and conjecture. We

should be laughed out of court if we came with such a story and such evidence."

"There is Sir Charles's death."

"Found dead without a mark upon him. You and I know that he died of sheer fright, and we know also what frightened him. But how are we to get twelve indifferent jurymen to know it? What signs are there of a hound?"

"Well, then, tonight?"

"We are not much better off tonight. Again, there was no direct connection between the hound and the man's death. No, my dear fellow; we must reconcile ourselves to the fact that we have no case at present, and that it is worth our while to run any risk in order to establish one."

"And how do you propose to do so?"

"I have great hopes of what Mrs. Laura Lyons may do for us when the position of affairs is made clear to her."

Watson could draw nothing further from him, and we walked, lost in thought, as far as the Baskerville gates.

"Are you coming up?"

"Yes; I see no reason for further concealment. But one last word, Watson. Say nothing of the hound to Sir Henry. Let him think that Selden's death was as Stapleton would have us believe. He will have a better nerve for the ordeal which he will have to undergo tomorrow, when he is engaged, if I remember your report aright, to dine with these people."

"And so am I."

"Then you must excuse yourself and he must go alone. That will be easily arranged. And now, if we are too late for dinner, I think that we are both ready for our suppers. And I believe that our young Septimus here is deserving of a special treat, in recognition of his own fine work on this evening."

* * *

SIR HENRY WAS MORE PLEASED THAN SURPRISED TO SEE SHERLOCK Holmes, for he had for some days been expecting that recent events would bring him down from London. He did raise his eyebrows, however, when he found that my master had neither any luggage nor any explanations for its absence.

Over a belated supper, Holmes and Watson explained to the baronet as much of our experience as it seemed desirable that he should know.

"I guess I should have some credit, for I have kept my promise," said the baronet. "If I hadn't sworn not to go about alone, I might have had a more lively evening, for I had a message from Stapleton asking me over there."

"I have no doubt that you would have had a more lively evening," said Holmes drily.

"But how about the case?" asked the baronet. "Have you made anything out of the tangle? I don't know that Watson and I are much the wiser since we came down."

"I think that I shall be in a position to make the situation rather more clear to you before long. It has been an exceedingly difficult and most complicated business. There are several points upon which we still want light—but it is coming together all the same."

"We've had one experience, as Watson has no doubt told you. We heard the hound on the moor, so I can swear that it is not all empty superstition. If you can muzzle that one and put him on a chain, I'll be ready to swear you are the greatest detective of all time."

"I think I will muzzle him and chain him all right if you will give me your help."

"Whatever you tell me to do I will do."

"Very good; and I will ask you also to do it blindly, without always asking the reason."

"Just as you like."

"If you will do this, I think the chances are that our little problem will soon be solved. I have no doubt."

He stopped suddenly and stared fixedly up over Watson's head into the air.

"Excuse the admiration of a connoisseur," said he as he waved his hand towards the line of portraits which covered the opposite wall. "Watson won't allow that I know anything of art, but that is mere jealousy because our views upon the subject differ. Now, these are a really very fine series of portraits."

"Well, I'm glad to hear you say so," said Sir Henry, glancing with some surprise at my master. "I don't pretend to know much about these things."

"I know what is good when I see it, and I see it now. That's a Kneller, I'll swear, that lady in the blue silk over yonder, and the stout gentleman with the wig ought to be a Reynolds. They are all family portraits, I presume?"

"Every one."

"Do you know the names?"

"Barrymore has been coaching me in them, and I think I can say my lessons fairly well."

"Who is the gentleman with the telescope?"

"That is Rear-Admiral Baskerville, who served under Rodney in the West Indies."

"And this Cavalier opposite to me—the one with the black velvet and the lace?"

"Ah, you have a right to know about him. That is the cause of all the mischief, the wicked Hugo, who started this whole Hound of the Baskervilles business. We're not likely to forget him."

"Dear me!" said Holmes. "He seems a quiet, meek-mannered man enough. I had pictured him as a more robust and ruffianly person."

"There's no doubt about the authenticity, for the name and the date, 1647, are on the back of the canvas."

Holmes said little more, but the picture of the old sinner

seemed to hold a fascination for him, and his eyes were continually fixed upon it during supper.

It was not until later, when Sir Henry had gone to his room, that Holmes was in a position to explain. He approached the portrait of the wicked Hugo.

"Do you see anything there? Is it like anyone you know?"

Watson gave it a long look. From my perspective, I saw where Holmes was headed, for once mentioned the similarity was immediately evident.

"Good heavens!" Watson finally cried in amazement. "Stapleton! But this is marvelous. It might be his portrait."

"Yes, a study of family portraits is enough to convert a man to the doctrine of reincarnation. The fellow is a Baskerville—that is evident."

"With designs upon the succession."

"Exactly," said Holmes. "This chance of the picture has supplied us with one of our most obvious missing links. We have him, Watson, we have him, and I dare swear that before tomorrow night he will be fluttering in our net as helpless as one of his own butterflies!"

He burst into one of his rare fits of laughter as he turned away from the picture. I have not heard him laugh often, and in my limited experience, it has always boded ill to somebody.

* * *

WATSON DISCOVERED US EARLY THE NEXT MORNING, AS HOLMES and I completed a long walk and stepped back into the large foyer of Baskerville Hall.

"Yes, we should have a full day today," Holmes remarked, and he rubbed his hands with the joy of action. "The nets are all in place."

"Have you been on the moor already?"

"Yes, Septimus and I were up with the sun. We have sent a

report from Grimpen to Princetown, as to the death of Selden. And I have also communicated with my faithful Cartwright, who would certainly have pined away at the door of my hut if I had not set his mind at rest about my safety."

"What is the next move?"

"To see Sir Henry. Ah, here he is!"

"Good-morning, Holmes," said the baronet. "You look like a general who is planning a battle."

"Just so. You are engaged, as I understand, to dine with our friends the Stapletons tonight?"

"I hope that you will come also. They are very hospitable people, and I am sure that they would be very glad to see you."

"I fear that we must go to London," said Holmes, indicating Watson and myself.

"To London?"

"Yes, I think that we should be more useful there at the present juncture."

The baronet's face perceptibly lengthened.

"I hoped that you were going to see me through this business. The Hall and the moor are not very pleasant places when one is alone."

"My dear fellow, you must trust me implicitly and do exactly what I tell you. You can tell your friends that we should have been happy to have come with you, but that urgent business required us to be in town. Will you remember to give them that message?"

"If you insist upon it."

"There is no alternative, I assure you."

I saw by the baronet's clouded brow that he was deeply troubled by what he regarded as our desertion.

"When do you desire to go?" he asked coldly.

"Immediately after breakfast. We will drive in to Coombe Tracey, but Watson will leave his things as a pledge that he will come back to you. Watson, you will send a note to Stapleton to tell him that you regret that you cannot come."

"I have a good mind to go to London with you," said the baronet. "Why should I stay here alone?"

"Because it is your post of duty. Because you gave me your word that you would do as you were told, and I tell you to stay."

"All right, then, I'll stay."

"One more direction! I wish you to drive to Merripit House. Send back your trap, however, and let them know that you intend to walk home."

"To walk across the moor?"

"Yes."

"But that is the very thing which you have so often cautioned me not to do."

"This time you may do it with safety. If I had not every confidence in your nerve and courage, I would not suggest it, but it is essential that you should do it."

"Then I will do it."

"And as you value your life do not go across the moor in any direction save along the straight path which leads from Merripit House to the Grimpen Road, and is your natural way home."

"I will do just what you say."

* * *

A COUPLE OF HOURS AFTERWARDS, WE WERE AT THE STATION OF Coombe Tracey and had dispatched the trap upon its return journey. A small boy was waiting upon the platform.

"Any orders, sir?"

"You will take this train to town, Cartwright. The moment you arrive, you will send a wire to Sir Henry Baskerville, in my name, to say that if he finds the pocketbook which I have dropped, he is to send it by registered post to Baker Street."

"Yes, sir."

"And ask at the station office if there is a message for me."

The boy returned with a telegram, which Holmes read aloud.

"'Wire received. Coming down with unsigned warrant. Arrive five- forty. Lestrade,'" he recited before folding the telegram and pocketing it.

"That is in answer to mine I sent this morning," continued Holmes. "He is the best of the professionals, I think, and we may need his assistance. Now, Watson, I think that we cannot employ our time better than by calling upon your acquaintance, Mrs. Laura Lyons."

* * *

MRS. LAURA LYONS WAS IN HER OFFICE. SHE SEEMED DELIGHTED TO see me and gave me much affection. Her interest in the two gentlemen who accompanied me, however, was clearly less effusive.

Sherlock Holmes opened his interview with a frankness and directness I had rarely observed in his dealings with women.

"I am investigating the circumstances which attended the death of the late Sir Charles Baskerville," said he. "My friend here, Dr. Watson, has informed me of what you have communicated, and also of what you have withheld in connection with that matter."

"What have I withheld?" she asked defiantly. She stopped petting me at once. I stepped toward her, to encourage its resumption, but Holmes had clearly unnerved her.

"You have confessed that you asked Sir Charles to be at the gate at ten o'clock. We know that that was the place and hour of his death. You have withheld what the connection is between these events."

"There is no connection."

"In that case the coincidence must indeed be an extraordinary one. I wish to be perfectly frank with you, Mrs. Lyons. We regard this case as one of murder, and the evidence may implicate not only your friend Mr. Stapleton, but his wife as well."

"His wife!" she cried.

"The fact is no longer a secret. The person who has passed for his sister is really his wife."

Mrs. Lyons had resumed her seat. Her hands were grasping the arms of her chair, and I saw that the pink nails had turned white with the pressure of her grip. At that moment, I was relieved it was the chair—and not me—that she was in contact with.

"His wife!" she said again. "His wife! He is not a married man."

Sherlock Holmes shrugged his shoulders.

"Prove it to me! And if you can do so—!"

The fierce flash of her eyes said more than any words.

"I have come prepared to do so," said Holmes, drawing several papers from his pocket. "Here is a photograph of the couple taken in York four years ago. It is indorsed 'Mr. and Mrs. Vandeleur,' but you will have no difficulty in recognizing him, and her also, if you know her by sight. Here are three written descriptions by trustworthy witnesses of Mr. and Mrs. Vandeleur, who at that time kept St. Oliver's private school."

She glanced at them, and then looked up at us with the set rigid face of a desperate woman.

"Mr. Holmes," said she, "this man had offered me marriage on condition that I could get a divorce from my husband. He has lied to me, the villain, in every conceivable way. Ask me what you like, and there is nothing which I shall hold back. One thing I swear to you, and that is that when I wrote the letter I never dreamed of any harm to the old gentleman, who had been my kindest friend."

"I entirely believe you, madam," said Sherlock Holmes. "The recital of these events must be very painful to you, and perhaps it will make it easier if I tell you what occurred, and you can check me if I make any material mistake. The sending of this letter was suggested to you by Stapleton?"

"He dictated it."

"I presume that the reason he gave was that you could receive help from Sir Charles for the legal expenses connected with your divorce?"

"Exactly."

"And then after you had sent the letter, he dissuaded you from keeping the appointment?"

"He told me that it would hurt his self-respect that any other man should find the money for such an object."

"And then you heard nothing until you read the reports of the death in the paper?"

"No."

"And he made you swear to say nothing about your appointment with Sir Charles?"

"He did. He said that the death was a very mysterious one, and that I should certainly be suspected if the facts came out. He frightened me into remaining silent."

"I think that on the whole you have made a fortunate escape," said Sherlock Holmes. "You have been walking for some months very near to the edge of a precipice. We must wish you good morning now, Mrs. Lyons, and it is probable that you will very shortly hear from us again."

* * *

WE MADE OUR WAY BACK TO THE TRAIN STATION AND STOOD ON THE platform.

"I shall soon be in the position of being able to put into a single connected narrative one of the most singular and sensational crimes of modern times," said Holmes as we stood waiting for the arrival of the express from town. "Students of criminology will remember the analogous incidents in Godno, in Little Russia, in the year '66, and of course there are the Anderson murders in North Carolina, but this case possesses some features which are entirely its own. Even now we have no clear case against this very wily man. But I shall be very much surprised if it is not clear enough before we go to bed this night."

The London express came roaring into the station, and a small, wiry bulldog of a man had sprung from a first-class carriage. The men all shook hands, and then Lestrade bent down and gave my head a welcoming pat. He looked up at Holmes.

"Anything good?" he asked.

"The biggest thing for years," said Holmes. "We have two hours before we need to begin. I think we might employ it in getting some dinner and then, Lestrade, we will take the London fog out of your throat by giving you a breath of the pure night air of Dartmoor. Never been there?"

"I have not, sir."

"Ah, well," said Holmes with a grin. "I don't suppose it is likely you will forget your first visit."

CHAPTER 15

One of Sherlock Holmes's defects—if, indeed, one may call it a defect—was that he was exceedingly loath to communicate his full plans until the instant of their fulfilment.

Partly it came, no doubt, from his own masterful nature, which loves to dominate and surprise those who are around him. Partly also from his professional caution, which urged him never to take any chances. The result, however, was very trying for those who were acting as his agents and assistants.

My nerves thrilled with anticipation when at last the cold wind upon my snout told me that we were back upon the moor. Every stride of the horses and every turn of the wheels was taking us nearer to our supreme adventure.

It was a relief to me when we at last passed Frankland's house and knew that we were drawing near to the Hall and to the scene of action. We did not drive up to the door but got down near the gate of the avenue. The wagonette was paid off and ordered to return to Coombe Tracey forthwith, while we started to walk to Merripit House.

"Are you armed, Lestrade?"

The little detective smiled. "As long as I have my trousers I have a hip-pocket, and as long as I have my hip-pocket, I have something in it."

"Good! Watson and I are also ready for emergencies."

"You're mighty close about this affair, Mr. Holmes. What's the game now?"

"A waiting game."

"My word, it does not seem a very cheerful place," said the police detective with a shiver, glancing round him at the gloomy slopes of the hill and at the huge lake of fog which lay over the Grimpen Mire. "I see the lights of a house ahead of us."

"That is Merripit House and the end of our journey. I must request you take a lesson from our friend, young Septimus here, to walk in complete silence."

We moved cautiously along the track as if we were bound for the house, but Holmes halted us when we were about two hundred yards from it.

"This will do," said he. "These rocks upon the right make an admirable screen."

"We are to wait here?"

"Yes, we shall make our little ambush here. Get into this hollow, Lestrade. You have been inside the house, have you not, Watson? Can you tell the position of the rooms? What are those latticed windows at this end?"

"I think they are the kitchen windows."

"And the one beyond, which shines so brightly?"

"That is certainly the dining-room."

"The blinds are up. You know the lie of the land best. Creep forward quietly and see what they are doing—but for heaven's sake don't let them know that they are being watched!"

Watson tiptoed down the path and I followed. He stooped behind the low wall which surrounded the stunted orchard. Creeping in its shadow, we reached a point whence we could look straight through the uncurtained window.

There were only two men in the room, Sir Henry and Stapleton. Both of them were smoking cigars, and coffee and wine were in front of them. Stapleton was talking with animation, but the baronet looked pale and distraught. Perhaps the thought of that lonely walk across the ill-omened moor was weighing heavily upon his mind.

As we watched them, Stapleton rose and left the room, while Sir Henry filled his glass again and leaned back in his chair, puffing at his cigar. I heard the creak of a door and the crisp sound of boots upon gravel. The steps passed along the path on the other side of the wall behind which I stood and Watson crouched.

Looking over, I saw the naturalist pause at the door of a shed in the corner of the orchard. A key turned in a lock, and as he passed into the shed, there was a curious scuffling noise from within. I sniffed the air, once again wishing for the helpful skills of Toby. There was an unfamiliar scent in the air, dank and dreadful, but I couldn't put more definition than that to it.

Stapleton was only a minute or so inside, and then I heard the key turn once more and he passed us and reentered the house. I saw him rejoin his guest, and we crept quietly back to where our companions were waiting to tell them what we had seen.

"You say, Watson, that the lady is not there?" Holmes asked when he had finished his report.

"No."

"Where can she be, then, since there is no light in any other room except the kitchen?"

"I cannot think where she is."

Over the great Grimpen Mire there hung a dense, white fog. It was drifting slowly in our direction and banked itself up like a wall on that side of us, low but thick and well defined. The moon shone on it, and it looked like a great shimmering ice-field. Holmes's face was turned towards it, and he muttered impatiently as he watched its sluggish drift.

"It's moving towards us."

"Is that serious?" whispered Watson.

"Very serious, indeed—the one thing upon earth which could have disarranged my plans. He can't be very long, now. It is already ten o'clock. Our success and even his life may depend upon his coming out before the fog is over the path."

The night was clear and fine above us. The stars shone cold and bright, while a half-moon bathed the whole scene in a soft, uncertain light.

Before us lay the dark bulk of the house, its serrated roof and bristling chimneys hard outlined against the sky. Broad bars of golden light from the lower windows stretched across the orchard and the moor. One of them was suddenly shut off. The servants had left the kitchen. There only remained the lamp in the dining-room where the two men—the murderous host and his guest—still chatted over their cigars.

Every minute that white woolly plain which covered one-half of the moor was drifting closer and closer to the house. Already the first thin wisps of it were curling across the golden square of the lighted window. The farther wall of the orchard was already invisible, and the trees were standing out of a swirl of white vapor.

As we watched it, the fog-wreaths came crawling round both corners of the house and rolled slowly into one dense bank. Holmes struck his hand passionately upon the rock in front of us and stamped his feet in his impatience.

"If he isn't out in a quarter of an hour, the path will be covered. In half an hour, we won't be able to see our hands in front of us."

"Shall we move farther back upon higher ground?"

"Yes, I think it would be as well."

So as the fog-bank flowed onward, we fell back before it until we were half a mile from the house, and still that dense white sea swept slowly and inexorably on.

"We are going too far," said Holmes. "We dare not take the chance of his being overtaken before he can reach us. At all costs we must hold our ground where we are." He dropped on his knees and clapped his ear to the ground. "Thank God, I think that I hear him coming."

A sound of quick steps broke the silence of the moor. Crouching among the stones, we stared intently at the silver-tipped bank in front of us. The steps grew louder, and through the fog, as through a curtain, there stepped the man whom we were awaiting.

He looked round him in surprise as he emerged into the clear, starlit night. Then he came swiftly along the path, passed close to where we lay, and went on up the long slope behind us. As he walked, he glanced continually over either shoulder, like a man who is ill at ease.

"Hist!" cried Holmes, and I heard the sharp click of a cocking pistol. "Look out! It's coming!"

There was a thin, crisp, continuous patter from somewhere in the heart of that crawling bank. The cloud was within fifty yards of where we lay, and we glared at it, uncertain what horror was about to break from the heart of it.

I was at Holmes's elbow, and I glanced for an instant at his face. It was pale and exultant, his eyes shining brightly in the moonlight. But suddenly they started forward in a rigid, fixed stare, and his lips parted in amazement. At the same instant, Lestrade gave a yell of terror and threw himself face downward upon the ground. I turned suddenly, my mind paralyzed by the dreadful shape which had sprung out upon us from the shadows of the fog.

A hound it was, an enormous coal-black hound, but not such a hound as I had ever seen. Fire burst from its open mouth, its eyes glowed with a smoldering glare, its muzzle was outlined in flick-ering flame. Never in the delirious dream of a disordered brain could anything more savage, more appalling, more hellish be conceived.

With long bounds, the huge black creature was leaping down

the track, following hard upon the footsteps of our friend. So paralyzed were the men by the apparition that they allowed him to pass before they had recovered their nerve.

I felt no such restriction and launched myself toward the creature, quickly gaining ground. The terrain was flat and for once I was able to put my speed to good use, galloping along and gaining on the beast.

Far away on the path I saw Sir Henry looking back, his face white in the moonlight, his hands raised in horror, glaring helplessly at the frightful thing which was hunting him down.

I put on a burst of speed, far surpassing any effort I might have ever displayed while coursing. No fox or hare had ever turned to see me moving at such a speed. I got alongside the beast and could feel the power of its muscles as it bore down on the baronet, who stood frozen in the path.

With a supreme effort, I passed the monstrous thing, brushing against its course, matted fur as I did. I put four, then five strides between us and then, sliding to a stop next to Sir Henry, I spun hard and rose up, barking and snarling at the charging brute.

His red eyes met mine and for just a flicker of a second I recognized madness in his gaze. He flicked his eyes from me to the man behind me and I took a step forward, increasing the ferocity of my barking. He froze in his tracks, his eyes showing the calculation that was processing behind them. I gave another loud snarl and took another step toward him, rising up on my back legs in preparation for diving headlong into this dark, feral creature. I could hear Sir Henry, whimpering behind me.

The beast pushed back on his haunches, launching himself directly at me, his mouth wide, his teeth bared and glowing. I matched his action, pushing off with my hind legs, prepared to meet him in mid-air.

A shot rang out. And then another.

The beast seemed to freeze in the air, his head turning toward the sound of the gunshot, a wail of agony issuing from his throat.

Three more shots and, with a last howl of agony and a vicious snap in the air, it fell upon its back, four feet pawing furiously. And then the legs fell limp upon its side.

I stepped back, still protecting Sir Henry behind me, as the men approached the fallen beast. Watson stooped, panting, and pressed his pistol to the dreadful, shimmering head, but it was useless to press the trigger. The giant hound was dead.

Sir Henry lay insensible where he had fallen.

"My God!" he whispered. "What was it? What, in heaven's name, was it?"

"It's dead, whatever it is," said Holmes. "We've laid the family ghost to rest once and forever."

In mere size and strength, it was a terrible creature which was lying stretched before us. It was not a pure bloodhound and it was not a pure mastiff; but it appeared to be a combination of the two —gaunt, savage, and as large as a small lioness. Even now in the stillness of death, the huge jaws seemed to be dripping with a bluish flame and the small, deep-set, cruel eyes were ringed with fire.

Watson placed his hand upon the glowing muzzle, and as he held them up, his fingers smoldered and gleamed in the darkness.

"Phosphorus," said he.

"A cunning preparation of it," said Holmes, sniffing at the dead animal. "There is no smell which might have interfered with his power of scent. We owe you a deep apology, Sir Henry, for having exposed you to this fright. I was prepared for a hound, but not for such a creature as this. And the fog gave us little time to receive him."

"You have saved my life."

"Having first endangered it. And, to be fair, Septimus bought us the necessary time to get here and fire a shot."

He gave me a firm pat on the head and then did a quick scan, to ensure I had received no wounds in the fray. Assured I was unharmed, he turned back to Sir Henry. "Are you strong enough to stand?"

"Yes, if you will help me up. What do you propose to do?"

"To leave you here. You are not fit for further adventures tonight. If you will wait, one or other of us will go back with you to the Hall."

He tried to stagger to his feet; but he was still ghastly pale and trembling in every limb. They helped him to a rock, where he sat shivering with his face buried in his hands.

"We must leave you now," said Holmes. "The rest of our work must be done, and every moment is of importance. We have our case, and now we only want our man.

* * *

"It's a thousand to one against our finding him at the house," said Holmes as we retraced our steps swiftly down the path. "Those shots must have told him that the game was up."

"We were some distance off, and this fog may have deadened them," suggested Watson.

"He followed the hound to call him off—of that you may be certain. No, no, he's gone by this time! But we'll search the house and make sure."

The front door was open, so we rushed in and hurried from room to room, to the amazement of a doddering old manservant who met us in the passage.

There was no light save in the dining-room, but Holmes caught up the lamp and left no corner of the house unexplored. No sign could we see of the man whom we were chasing. On the upper floor, however, one of the bedroom doors was locked.

"There's someone in here," cried Lestrade. "I can hear a movement. Open this door!"

A faint moaning and rustling came from within. Holmes

struck the door just over the lock with the flat of his foot and it flew open. Pistol in hand, we all rushed into the room.

But there was no sign within it of that desperate and defiant villain whom we expected to see. Instead we were faced by an object so strange and so unexpected that we stood for a moment staring at it in amazement.

The room had been fashioned into a small museum, and the walls were lined by a number of glass-topped cases full of that collection of butterflies and moths.

In the center of this room there was an upright beam. To this post, a figure was tied, so swathed and muffled in the sheets which had been used to secure it that one could not for the moment tell whether it was that of a man or a woman.

In a minute we had torn off the gag, unswathed the bonds, and Mrs. Stapleton sank upon the floor in front of us.

"The brute!" cried Holmes. "Here, Lestrade, your brandy-bottle! Put her in the chair! She has fainted from ill-usage and exhaustion."

She opened her eyes again.

"Is he safe?" she asked. "Has he escaped?"

"He cannot escape us, madam."

"No, no, I did not mean my husband. Sir Henry? Is he safe?"

"Yes."

"And the hound?"

"It is dead."

She gave a long sigh of satisfaction.

"Thank God! Thank God! Oh, this villain! See how he has treated me!" She shot her arms out from her sleeves, and we saw with horror that they were all covered with bruises. "I know now that I have been his dupe and his tool." She broke into passionate sobbing as she spoke.

"Tell us then where we shall find him," said Holmes. "If you have ever aided him in evil, help us now and so atone."

"There is but one place where he can have fled," she answered. "There is an old tin mine on an island in the heart of the mire. It was there that he kept his hound and there also he had made preparations so that he might have a refuge. That is where he would fly."

The fog-bank lay like white wool against the window. Holmes held the lamp towards it.

"No one could find his way into the Grimpen Mire tonight."

She laughed and clapped her hands. Her eyes and teeth gleamed with fierce merriment.

"He may find his way in, but never out," she cried. "How can he see the guiding wands tonight? We planted them together, he and I, to mark the pathway through the mire. Oh, if I could only have plucked them out today. Then indeed you would have had him at your mercy!"

It was evident to us that all pursuit was in vain until the fog had lifted.

We left Lestrade in possession of the house, while Holmes, Watson and I went back with the baronet to Baskerville Hall. The story of the Stapletons could no longer be withheld from him, but he took the blow bravely when he learned the truth about the woman whom he had loved.

But the shock of the night's adventures had shattered his nerves, and before morning he lay delirious in a high fever under the care of Dr. Mortimer.

* * *

ON THE MORNING AFTER THE DEATH OF THE HOUND, THE FOG HAD lifted and we were guided by Mrs. Stapleton to the point where they had found a pathway through the bog.

We left her standing upon the thin peninsula of firm, peaty soil, which tapered out into the widespread bog. Rank reeds and lush, slimy water-plants sent an odor of decay and a heavy vapor onto our faces, while a false step plunged us more than once into the dark, quivering mire, which shook for yards in soft undulations around our feet.

Once only we saw a trace that someone had passed that perilous way before us. From amid a tuft of cotton grass, some dark thing was projecting. Holmes held an old black boot in the air.

"'Meyers, Toronto' is printed on the leather inside," said he. "It is our friend Sir Henry's missing boot."

"Thrown there by Stapleton in his flight," suggested Watson.

"Exactly. He used it to set the hound upon the track. He fled when he knew the game was up, still clutching it. And he hurled it away at this point of his flight. We know at least that he came so far in safety."

But more than that we were never destined to know, though there was much which we might surmise. There was no chance of finding footsteps in the mire, for the rising mud oozed swiftly in upon them, but as we at last reached firmer ground beyond the morass, we all looked eagerly for new foot prints. But no slightest sign of them ever met our eyes.

"If the earth tells a true story," said Holmes, "then Stapleton never reached that island of refuge towards which he struggled through the fog last night. Somewhere in the heart of the great Grimpen Mire, down in the foul slime of the huge morass, this cold and cruel-hearted man is forever buried.

"I said it in London, Watson, and I say it again now," continued Holmes, "that never yet have we helped to hunt down a more dangerous man than he who is lying yonder."

He swept his long arm towards the huge green-splotched bog which stretched away until it merged into the auburn slopes of the moor.

CHAPTER 16

*I*t was the end of a raw and foggy November night, and I lay upon the hearth-rug before a blazing fire in our sitting-room in Baker Street.

Holmes sat in one chair, methodically filling his pipe, while Watson sat in another, finishing that day's papers. He folded the sheets and set them aside before looking over at Holmes.

"Since some time has passed," said Watson, "I am wondering if I might induce you to discuss the details of the Baskerville mystery."

The topic might seemed to have appeared out of the blue, but Sir Henry and Dr. Mortimer were in London, on their way to that long voyage which had been recommended for the restoration of his shattered nerves. They had called upon us that very afternoon, so that it was natural that the subject should come up for discussion.

"The whole course of events," said Holmes, "from the point of view of the man who called himself Stapleton, was simple and direct. Although, to us, it all appeared exceedingly complex.

"My inquiries show beyond all question that the family portrait did not lie, and that this fellow was indeed a Baskerville," continued Holmes. "He was a son of that Rodger Baskerville, the younger brother of Sir Charles, who fled with a sinister reputation to South America, where he was said to have died unmarried. He did, as a matter of fact, marry, and had one child.

"This fellow, whose real name is the same as his father's, married Beryl and, having purloined a considerable sum of public money, changed his name to Vandeleur and fled to England, posing as a teacher. The school, which had begun well, sank from disrepute into infamy. The Vandeleurs found it convenient to change their name to Stapleton, and he brought the remains of his fortune, his schemes for the future, and his taste for entomology to the south of England.

"The fellow had evidently made inquiry and found that only two lives intervened between him and a valuable estate. When he went to Devonshire his plans were, I believe, exceedingly hazy. But that he meant mischief from the first is evident from the way in which he took his wife with him in the character of his sister. The idea of using her as a decoy was clearly already in his mind, though he may not have been certain how the details of his plot were to be arranged.

"He meant in the end to have the estate, and he was ready to use any tool or run any risk for that end. His first act was to establish himself as near to his ancestral home as he could, and his second was to cultivate a friendship with Sir Charles Baskerville and with the neighbors.

"The baronet himself told him about the family hound, and so prepared the way for his own death. Stapleton, as I will continue to call him, knew that the old man's heart was weak and that a shock would kill him. His ingenious mind instantly suggested a way by which the baronet could be done to death, and yet it would be hardly possible to bring home the guilt to the real murderer.

"Having conceived the idea, he proceeded to carry it out with considerable finesse. The use of artificial means to make the creature diabolical was a flash of genius upon his part. The dog he bought in London from Ross and Mangles, the dealers in Fulham Road. It was the strongest and most savage in their possession. He had already on his insect hunts learned to penetrate the Grimpen Mire, and so had found a safe hiding-place for the creature. Here he kenneled it and waited his chance.

"He had hoped that his wife might lure Sir Charles to his ruin, but here she proved unexpectedly independent. She would not endeavor to entangle the old gentleman in a sentimental attachment which might deliver him over to his enemy. Threats and even, I am sorry to say, blows refused to move her.

"He found a way out of his difficulties through the unfortunate woman, Mrs. Laura Lyons. By representing himself as a single man, he acquired complete influence over her, and he gave her to understand that in the event of her obtaining a divorce from her husband he would marry her. His plans were suddenly brought to a head by his knowledge that Sir Charles was about to leave the Hall. He therefore put pressure upon Mrs. Lyons to write this letter, imploring the old man to give her an interview on the evening before his departure for London. He then, by a specious argument, prevented her from going, and so had the chance for which he had waited.

"Driving back in the evening from Coombe Tracey, he was in time to get his hound, to treat it with his infernal paint, and to bring the beast round to the gate at which he had reason to expect that he would find the old gentleman waiting. The dog, incited by its master, sprang over the wicket-gate and pursued the unfortunate baronet, who fled screaming down the yew alley. He fell dead at the end of the alley from heart disease and terror. The hound had kept upon the grassy border while the baronet had run down the path, so that no track but the man's was visible.

"On seeing him lying still, the creature had probably approached to sniff at him, but finding him dead had turned away again. It was then that it left the print which was actually observed by Dr. Mortimer. The hound was called off and hurried away to its lair in the Grimpen Mire, and a mystery was left which puzzled the authorities, alarmed the countryside, and finally brought the case within the scope of our observation."

"Fascinating," said Watson. "Devilishly cunning, that. It would be almost impossible to make a case against the real murderer. His only accomplice was one who could never give him away."

"Yes, and the grotesque, inconceivable nature of the device only served to make it more effective."

"But at that point, was Stapleton aware of the existence of an heir in Canada?"

"I do not know," said Holmes. "But in any case, he would very soon learn it from his friend Dr. Mortimer."

Holmes had succeeded in filling his pipe and the next few moments were spent in silence, as he lit it.

"My guess is that Stapleton's first idea was that this young stranger from Canada might possibly be done to death in London without coming down to Devonshire at all," continued Holmes.

"He distrusted his wife ever since she had refused to help him in laying a trap for the old man, and he dared not leave her long out of his sight, for fear he should lose his influence over her. It was for this reason that he took her to London with him. Here he kept his wife imprisoned in her room while he, disguised in a beard, followed Dr. Mortimer to Baker Street and afterwards to the station and to the Northumberland Hotel.

"His wife had such a fear of her husband—a fear founded upon brutal ill-treatment—that she dare not write to warn the man whom she knew to be in danger. Eventually, as we know, she adopted the expedient of cutting out the words which would form the message, and addressing the letter in a disguised hand. It reached the baronet, and gave him the first warning of his danger."

"And then there was the business with the boot," added Watson.

"Yes, it was essential for Stapleton to get some article of Sir Henry's attire so that, in case he was driven to use the dog, he might always have the means of setting him upon his track. By chance, however, the first boot which was procured for him was a new one and, therefore, useless for his purpose.

"He then had it returned and obtained another—a most instructive incident, since it proved conclusively to my mind that we were dealing with a real hound, as no other supposition could explain this anxiety to obtain an old boot and this indifference to a new one."

"Clever devil," grumbled Watson.

"Indeed. We had an example of his readiness of resource that one morning when he got away from us so successfully, and also of his audacity in sending back my own name to me through the cabman. From that moment, he understood that I had taken over the case in London, and that therefore there was no chance for him there. He returned to Dartmoor and awaited the arrival of the baronet."

"The Stapletons then went down to Devonshire, where they were soon followed by you, Sir Henry and Septimus. I followed soon thereafter. It was my game to watch Stapleton. It was evident, however, that I could not do this if I were with you, since he would be keenly on his guard.

"By the time that you discovered me upon the moor, I had a complete knowledge of the whole business, but I had no case which could go to a jury. Even Stapleton's attempt upon Sir Henry that night, which ended in the death of the unfortunate convict, did not help us much in proving murder against our man.

"There seemed to be no alternative but to catch him red-handed, and to do so we had to use Sir Henry, alone and apparently unprotected, as bait. We did so, and at the cost of a severe shock to our client we succeeded in completing our case and driving Stapleton to his destruction."

"And save his wife in the process."

"Yes. He tied her up that she might have no chance of warning Sir Henry. He hoped, no doubt, that when the whole countryside put down the baronet's death to the curse of his family, he could win his wife back and that she would keep silent upon what she knew.

"There only remains one difficulty," said Watson. "If Stapleton came into the succession, how could he explain the fact that he, the heir, had been living unannounced under another name so close to the property?"

"It is a formidable difficulty, and I fear that you ask too much when you expect me to solve it. Mrs. Stapleton has heard her husband discuss the problem on several occasions. There were three possible courses.

"He might claim the property from South America, establish his identity before the British authorities there and so obtain the fortune without ever coming to England at all. Or he might adopt an elaborate disguise during the short time that he need be in London. Or, again, he might furnish an accomplice with the proofs and papers, putting him in as heir, and retaining a claim upon some proportion of his income. We cannot doubt from what we know of him that he would have found some way out of the difficulty."

"Based on what we've learned about him, I think you are correct."

"And now, I think our friend Septimus here is due for a long walk," said Holmes as he glanced out the window. "Despite the cold and the rain, I suspect it may be just the thing."

He looked down at me. I glanced at the window, to confirm the dismal weather report, and then turned my head, burying it into my haunch, indicating that a walk was not part of my current agenda.

I think he stood there for several long moments, leash in hand, before finally giving up.

"Well, Watson, what do you say to dinner at Mancini's? It's but a short cab ride away and I might even be induced to bring back some slices of beef or a fine bone for our reluctant friend here."

I listened while they bundled up and stomped out, hoping he had not been taunting me with that offer of leftovers.

With that, I shut my eyes and slipped quickly into a warm and inviting slumber.

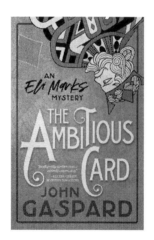

THE AMBITIOUS CARD
An Eli Marks Mystery (#1)
The life of a magician isn't all kiddie shows and card tricks.
Sometimes it's murder. Especially when magician Eli Marks very
publicly debunks a famed psychic, and said psychic ends up dead.
The evidence, including a bloody King of Diamonds playing card
(one from Eli's own Ambitious Card routine), directs the police
right to Eli.

As more psychics are slain, and more King cards rise to the top, Eli can't escape suspicion. Things get really complicated when romance blooms with a beautiful psychic, and Eli discovers she's the next target for murder, and he's scheduled to die with her. Now Eli must use every trick he knows to keep them both alive and reveal the true killer.

ALSO BY JOHN GASPARD

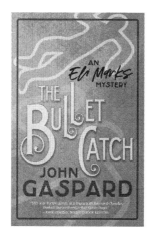

THE BULLET CATCH
An Eli Marks Mystery (#2)
Newly-single magician Eli Marks reluctantly attends his high
school reunion against his better judgment, only to become
entangled in two deadly encounters with his former classmates.
The first is the fatal mugging of an old crush's husband, followed
by the suspicious deaths of the victim's business associates.

At the same time, Eli also comes to the aid of a classmate-turned-movie-star who fears that attempting The Bullet Catch in an upcoming movie may be his last performance. As the bodies begin to pile up, Eli comes to the realization that juggling these murderous situations – while saving his own neck – may be the greatest trick he's ever performed.

ALSO BY JOHN GASPARD

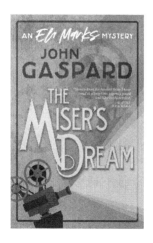

THE MISER'S DREAM
An Eli Marks Mystery (#3)
A casual glance out his apartment window turns magician Eli
Marks' life upside down. After spotting a dead body in the
projection booth of the movie theater next door, Eli is pulled into
the hunt for the killer. As he attempts to puzzle out a solution to
this classic locked room mystery, he must deal with a crisis of a
more personal nature: the appearance of a rival magician who

threatens not only Eli's faith in himself as a performer, but his relationship with his girlfriend.

But the killer won't wait and starts taking homicidal steps to bring Eli's investigation to a quick and decisive end. Things get even worse when his magician rival offers his own plausible solution to the mystery. With all the oddball suspects gathered together, Eli must unveil the secrets to this movie-geek whodunit or find himself at the wrong end of the trick.

ALSO BY JOHN GASPARD

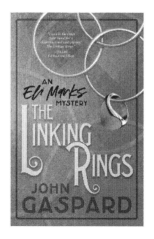

THE LINKING RINGS
An Eli Marks Mystery (#4)

Eli's trip to London with his uncle Harry quickly turns homicidal when the older magician finds himself accused of murder. A second slaying does little to take the spotlight off Harry. Instead it's clear someone is knocking off Harry's elderly peers in bizarrely effective ways. But who? The odd gets odder when the prime suspect appears to be a bitter performer with a grudge...who committed suicide over thirty years before. While Eli struggles to prove his uncle's innocence--and keep them both alive--he finds himself embroiled in a battle of his own: a favorite magic routine of his has been ripped off by another hugely popular magician.

ALSO BY JOHN GASPARD

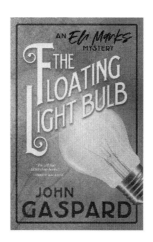

THE FLOATING LIGHT BULB
An Eli Marks Mystery (#5)
When a magician is murdered in the midst of his act at the Mall of
America, Eli Marks is asked to step in and take over the daily
shows--while also keeping his eyes and ears open for clues about
this bizarre homicide.
As Eli combs the maze-like corridors beneath the Mall of
America's massive amusement park looking for leads, he also

struggles to learn and perform an entirely new magic act. Meanwhile, the long-time watering hole for Uncle Harry and his Mystics pals is closing. So in addition to the murder investigation and the new act, Eli must help the grumpy (and picky) seniors find a suitable new hang out.

ALSO BY JOHN GASPARD

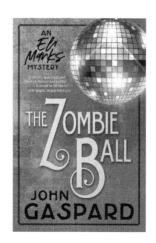

THE ZOMBIE BALL

An Eli Marks Mystery (#6)

Eli's asked to perform his magic act at a swanky charity gala, *The Zombie Ball* – a former zombie pub crawl which has grown into an annual high-class social event. What begins as a typical stage show for Eli turns deadly when two of the evening's sponsors are found murdered under truly unusual circumstances. Compounding this drama is the presence of Eli's ex-wife and her new husband, Homicide Detective Fred Hutton. Under pressure to solve the crime before the 800 guests depart, Eli and his detective nemesis go head-to-head to uncover the bizarre clues that will unravel this macabre mystery.

ALSO BY JOHN GASPARD

THE RIPPEROLOGISTS

The Ripperologists is a contemporary thriller about two competing experts who are forced to work together to beat the clock when a copycat serial killer begins recreating Jack the Ripper's 1888 murder spree.

Set against the backdrop of the fascinating subculture of

Ripperologists, the story takes equal stabs at the disparate worlds of publishing, Ripper studies, fan conventions, and Internet chatrooms, as our two unlikely heroes employ their (often contrary) knowledge of a 120-year-old phantom to hunt down a modern killer.

ABOUT THE AUTHOR

Originally a physician, Arthur Conan Doyle published *A Study in Scarlet* in 1887, the first of four novels about Sherlock Holmes and Dr. Watson.

His version of *The Hound of the Baskervilles* was first published in 1901. In addition, Doyle wrote over fifty short stories featuring the famous detective.

He died in 1930 of a heart attack and was buried in the rose garden at his home, Windlesham Manor.

ABOUT THE OTHER AUTHOR

John Gaspard is the author of the popular *Eli Marks* mystery series, about a working magician who stumbles into murder cases.

In real life, John's not a magician, but he has directed a bunch of low-budget features that cost very little and made even less – and that's no small trick. He's also written multiple books on the subject of low-budget filmmaking. Ironically, they've made more than the films.

He's also written for TV and the stage.

John lives in Minnesota and shares his home with his lovely wife, one or more greyhounds, a few cats and a handful of pet allergies.